HANGING ON FOR DEAR LIFE . . .

I didn't so much decide to climb back down as my wedged knee and my grip on the peak of the fence began to slip their hold and let gravity have its way with me.

I sat where I had dropped, trying to decide whether I had learned my lesson now or was determined to risk life and limb again to get a closer look at whatever was going on in the second story of that house.

Walk away? That'd be new.

Besides, this brilliantly lit mansion had become a kind of nose-thumbing symbol to me, perched on its peak, shielded by laws of privacy, flaunting whatever was going on there, legal or not. Already I'd seen two women I cared about—one a mere girl—go into that fortress dressed like call girls. . . . I was going to find out just what they were being expected to do there. . . .

Books by Patricia Brooks

Falling from Grace
But for the Grace

A Molly Piper Mystery

But for the Grace

Patricia Brooks

A Dell Book

Published by
Dell Publishing
a division of
Random House, Inc.
1540 Broadway
New York, New York 10036

ISBN: 0-440-22608-2

Printed in the United States of America

Published simultaneously in Canada

May 2000

10 9 8 7 6 5 4 3 2 1

OPM

*To Mary Jo Isenmann
and the many angels of the
Coupeville United Methodist Church
for keeping me spiritually
and emotionally alive
during the writing
of this book.*

MANY THANKS
to Rain, my reader,
Carol McCleary, my agent,
Mitch Hoffman, my editor,
and Kathy Lord, my copy editor,
for their right-on suggestions and
unerring catches of dropped stitches.

CHAPTER
1

THE WANTED POSTER appeared at the corner of Parsley and Primrose on December 29.

The location was a logical choice, Parsley Street being the primary thoroughfare—all four blocks of it—along the face of the village of Grace, on Prince Island, off the Washington coast. Most trafficked by residents and tourists alike, the site would ensure maximum humiliation for the poster's unlikely target: the eminent Edmond Anderson Bercain, then-president of the East Island Chamber of Commerce.

The timing of the posting was no accident either: That corner put it dead in the path of the upcoming Saints and Sinners Parade, the much-anticipated New Year's Eve event conceived by Grace's new Tourist Bureau chief, Hugh Gidoux. A transplant from New Orleans, Gidoux had promised Grace its own mini-Mardi Gras—soon to become, said he, a lucrative Prince Island tradition. What better time and place to embarrass one of the community's major pillars?

Grace is known for its elegantly artsy style, and the Parsley Street NOTICES board is a prime example. No raw square of cork on a post, the foot-long magnetic scroll is tucked beneath the hammered-metal elbow of a pint-size nineteenth-century messenger boy, complete with cropped jacket and cap. The black silhouette tops a fluted iron post confiscated from the burned ruins of one of the village's first and finest Victorian houses, now recreated as a real-estate office at Nutmeg and Rose.

Positioned as the board is in front of Colleen's Cut 'N Curl and overseen by Mayor Marion Stephenson-Roth, proprietor of the Sweet Scents shop next door, not much gets posted there that escapes the censor's eye. But I passed the corner early, just after seven that morning, so the censors had not yet gathered.

The photo displayed was a publicity shot familiar from regular exposure in the *Grace Guardian*: Bercain as host of the Charity Ball; Bercain as chair of the Chamber of Commerce; Bercain as candidate for mayor, rumored as a stepping-stone to his true destination: the governor's mansion. Apparently, someone(s) had decided that Edmond Bercain's press was too uniformly flattering and in need of balance.

WANTED FOR CRIMES AGAINST THE PEOPLE, the poster read in bold thirty-point caps above the picture.

Despite the jocularity of the price put on Bercain's patrician head (2¢), the *crimes* enumerated below appeared more serious:

1. For *the theft of jobs from Prince Islanders and the exploitation of Haitian workers.*
2. For *evasion of rightful taxation.*
3. For *domestic crimes of omission and commission.*
4. For *a cowardly act from his sinful, duplicitous past.*

The accusing group, signing itself *The Liberation Brigade*, went on to add bite to its bark. According to the poster, the Brigade had *liberated* certain objects from Bercain's possession and returned them to their *rightful owners*. These included some twenty-eight ivory carvings *illegally harvested from African elephants*, which were being returned to Africa's Ivory Coast. Three sizable Persian carpets, woven by *enslaved children*, would be donated to a Pakistani orphanage. And Northwest Indian arts and crafts—for which, the poster charged, their artisans had been *shamefully underpaid*—would be returned to the original tribes.

To have *liberated* such objects, I realized, the Brigade must have burgled Bercain's home. A felony. Tut-tut. But I couldn't seem to get the smile off my face as I jogged the rest of the way down Parsley Street toward the stairway to the beach. Bercain would be pissed. As would the mayor, Maid Marion—not two of my favorite pretentious people.

Unseemly thoughts for a private investigator, to be sure. On the ladder of law enforcement, a P.I. is only a rung or two below a police officer. And I'd been that too, for more than a year in Chicago, before a bullet brought early retirement from the force and one after another unsatisfying substitute jobs.

But let's face it: As a detective, public or private, I don't exactly fit the mold. Twenty-seven is young in the biz, and females still a game minority. But it's my height that draws the stares: Four-foot-nine is just right for a serious gymnast, which I was for nine of my early years, but it defies expectations if you're looking for someone to solve your thorniest problems.

Those stats do, however, tend to make me identify with the underdog, as this Brigade seemed to. I've always thought of myself as a sixties person born too late. Issues seemed so clear-cut black-and-white back then, and guts were all you needed to make your mark for justice. Guts are one thing I've got. More than good sense, some have said. Okay, many have said.

I paused at the top of the bluff separating the village from the waterfront, beside the statue of Captain Pyrus, rendered life-size in weathered brass at the rail, his telescope trained on the shipping lanes of the Saratoga Passage. Pyrus was credited with "founding" the island when his ship ran aground here early in the nineteenth century. It had been named Pyrus Island in his honor, but that had been bastardized to "Pirates" by the sixties exiles from the Haight, who gained a majority in Grace and proceeded to rename the streets in true flower-child tradition: flowers for the north–south, herbs for the east–west. Soon most everyone—at least on the East Island—was using the name, until the more conservative residents of the rest of the island resolved to eliminate the "Pirates" temptation and renamed it Prince Island, boosting property taxes as befitted royalty.

I looked at the sky, a horizontal canvas of gray-on-gray layers of cloud cover, the lights on the mainland still brighter than the dawn. A chilly rain looked imminent, but I continued anyway, jouncing down the series of wooden switchback stairs to a grassy strip set with picnic tables, inviting a comfortable stop for contemplation of the coastline.

A further set of ten lichen-slick concrete steps—without handrails—descended the rest of the way to the beach, but that venture was not encouraged. A black-on-white metal commercial sign warned PROCEED AT YOUR OWN RISK. I did, of course, proceed.

Usually, I run in the mornings in the woods that surround my camper, which is parked behind the cottage of my friend Free. There being no ready-made path in that portion of Shepherd's Woods, I'd forged one, studding my run with obligatory leaps over fallen logs, drops into gulches, and zigzags around piles of brush and thorny bushes. The constant vigilance required probably reduces the endorphins that are supposed to be one of the perks of running, but I consider it part of my training as a private detective, a trade I've plied on the island for the past year and a half.

The morning in question, though, I'd had to get in to my office early, to call Nate Paulsen, a New York P.I. recommended by my mentor, Simon Emmershaw, himself a semi-retired P.I. in Olympia, on the mainland. I had a client with some missing bonds that he wanted traced discreetly, since the thief was most likely his errant son. Paulsen had, Simon told me, an inside track to the world of high finance; if he'd help I could save myself a trip and my client the fare. Eight years in Chicago, first in college, then at work, had given me my fill of big cities for a while. I was enjoying my island.

On the beach the tide was nearly in, leaving only the mottled gray-brown upper shore, studded with large white-barnacled rocks and their offspring. Past the roughness, I kicked off my shoes and hit my favorite running surface: the fine sand at the water's edge, firm as a tongue.

That morning, though, my beach run was cut short. I generally jog about a mile along the beach, from the Parsley Street steps around a rocky point to Grace Bay, where a small collection of modest crafts bobs patiently on both sides of a ten-foot pier. When the King's Castle luxury resort went in on the western edge of town—a hotly contested venture—Grace's public beach was cut by a third. Now, the sign straight ahead of me—PRIVATE NO TRESPASSING—indicated that the democratically available beach was shrinking even further.

I jogged in place, glaring at the sign as though it had printed itself. This was too much. From nearly eighty miles of perimeter sand when the first white settlers had come to the island, the public beaches had shrunk to six by the time I arrived. And the number was still dwindling, as developers dropped money in the right places for permits to sell water-front properties to private homeowners who wanted their ocean views uncluttered by pesky pedestrians.

Never one to pay much mind to prohibitions, I trotted on past the sign, looking for its source. Just beyond the point was a sheer escarpment, and I rounded it to see, on a lofty slate ledge, a structure that hadn't been there only a month or two before.

The luxurious house gave me the eerie feeling that it had sprung full-blown from the rock—Venus on the half-cliff. Two stories topped by a turret with a widow's walk, the house had a fat sweep of deck that rounded the whole like the gesture of a flourishing arm. Its blinding white paint made the place look like a glittering grand piano that would have done Liberace proud.

The deck's periphery was studded with lampposts, ugly industrial aluminum poles topped by floodlights like the faceted eyes of insects, all trained on their little bite of the beach. I half expected to see a *Sunset*-magazine–endorsed barbecue pit at their focal point on the sand. Maybe next week.

I couldn't see a second sign signaling the end of the private zone, but that was pretty irrelevant: this stretch of beach dead-ends below Aster and Sunflower, about half a mile south. There'd been talk for years of making another stairway access there, but I guessed the private sector had gotten there first. Again. My mood soured, I backtracked; I would run the blocks back to my office instead of using them for cooldown. Already it was looking like an aborted day; Paulsen hadn't been there either.

Before I climbed the steps, though, I made my usual stop to consult The Faces, my personal oracles.

No one seems to know when the faces were carved into the seawall below Grace, or by what hand. They appear timeless, as old as the stone itself. The uncanny thing, though, is how identical they seem to be. Androgynous and highly stylized in the Native American tradition, the faces have the same falls of bound hair on either side, deep-cut flaring eyebrows over slanted eyes rising to a point. The cheeks are decorated with a pattern like open hands on either side of the nose, and the big-lipped mouths are wide, almost rectangular, above a strong chin.

Only the uneven hand of the wind has served to differentiate them, the sea's salt settling in the crevices of the faces in somewhat different patterns. On one, a white stripe falls straight from the forehead to the chin, giving the face a righteous, challenging aspect, the face of a warrior. On another, the white has filled the eyes, like light—the face, perhaps, of a seer. On that visage the white arc above the mouth gives a benign expression, while on another, the line of white extends just that much farther on either side of the mouth that it turns down, giving the face a grim, morose appearance.

I usually pause in my run before them, marveling at the sameness, the effects of the small points of difference. I look for traces of emotion I might have missed, and as often as not I find them, sometimes differing from visit to visit. Pure projection, any psychologist would tell you, but strangely compelling. I have been known to go to the beach just for the consultation.

That day, though, they appeared to be keeping their secrets to themselves, and I jogged up the steps to Parsley Street with a gutful of frustration. My beach run had been irreparably foreshortened; next I'd find the woods fenced.

When I reached Primrose, the WANTED poster was gone too. So much for the spirit of revolution, Grace-style, I thought.

I had no idea.

CHAPTER
2

I THOUGHT LITTLE MORE about the WANTED poster over that day and the next. I'd reached Paulsen and he had gone to considerable trouble to trace the bonds. Whereupon my client informed me that he no longer wished to pursue the matter. He didn't give a reason, but I pictured the home-coming of the prodigal son, forgiveness flowing like the blood of the fatted calf. I billed him for my services and those of Paulsen—at New York rates—and turned my attention to my other current case, an AWOL husband going down for his third count. I just hoped his wife would stick to her guns this time, so this search, too, wouldn't have to be redone in another six months. You can get real cynical in this job.

The flyers had not entirely disappeared. That first after-noon, when I stopped by The Blue Heron for lunch, the no-tice was posted on the street-level door and again two flights up on the café's bulletin board. I also noticed it tacked to a telephone pole at the intersection of Crest Drive and Wolf Road on my way out of town. Still, I was more than sur-prised to find Edmond Bercain waiting for me when I arrived at my office December 31.

Oddly, my first thought upon seeing him above me on the staircase landing was that he didn't lose much in a black-and-white photograph. A man of medium build, with medium-brown hair and medium-brown eyes, only his haughty expression and the fine tailoring of his gray pin-striped three-piece seemed to distinguish him from any man in any crowd.

He made an inauspicious beginning as I neared the landing, saying through a scowl, "You have no home phone." His tone suggested a serious breach of etiquette.

"No," I replied, adding silently, *and this is why*.

But I contented myself with an arched eyebrow and silent eye contact several moments beyond polite. (I had re-hearsed this look in the mirror; I wasn't a theater major for nothing.) Then I unlocked the door and stepped aside, gesturing for him to enter.

"Won't you have a seat, Mr. Bercain," I said, indicating the shabby but comfortable client chair.

But he shook his head impatiently, foiling my intent to get his head lower than mine. So I rounded my oversize desk and seated myself, without removing my windbreaker, wishing I'd known to dress for this encounter in other than my usual sweatshirt and jeans.

It could be worse, I told myself: I could be wearing the one that read: *Good girls go to heaven. Bad girls go everywhere*.

"You've seen the posters," Bercain said, a sharpness in his tone that suggested complicity.

It wasn't a question, so I only nodded.

"I want it stopped. I want to know who's responsible, and I want it stopped."

Then he answered my unasked question. "Chief Belgium said you could be trusted, that you'd handled that Holman . . . situation with discretion."

Since that case had climaxed with my action photo splattered over the front pages of half the newspapers in the state, I was surprised at the word *discretion*. But maybe he meant only my restraint in not sharing all the family's dirty laundry with the media.

"Also, you probably know those Squatters. I understand you live in the woods yourself."

I fought a smile. My camper dwelling must have seemed to him as close to a state of vagrancy as the tent city of the Squatters, the media's name for some dozen-or-so islanders who'd recently lost their homesteads to inflated property taxes, brought on by the flood of Seattle commuters/ weekenders/snowbirds who'd flocked to the island in the last decade and paid top dollar for land once modestly held. Refusing to leave the island, the now-homeless had set up camp in Shepherd's Woods last spring and had resisted all efforts to evict them. The woods at least, they said, were public property, and they were the public.

"I take it you believe this Brigade and the Squatter folk are one and the same?" I asked Bercain.

"Of course. Who else could it be?"

Whereupon he crossed to the client chair and sat on the edge of its seat, frowning at his perfectly manicured fingernails. "It's all economics of course," he said. "Those who sit on their butts and therefore have not, turning against those of us who've worked like hell to make something for ourselves."

I missed his next words, thinking how interesting it was that he'd said *for* rather than the customary *of* ourselves.

". . . not going to be slandered by a bunch of hoodlums," he concluded, fixing me with an intense look that seemed to deepen the brown in his small eyes.

Time for me to stand, I decided, exert whatever height I had. As I did, I half-turned toward the window behind me, gazing down Dahlia Street to the small sliver of Grace Bay my overpriced view afforded me. The sight brought to mind the newly foreshortened beach, and a momentary cloud seemed to cross the bright morning sky.

"Were there other items stolen besides those mentioned on the flyer?" I asked.

"As though their common thievery was some sort of Robin Hood prank," Bercain growled.

I turned to see him rearranging his expression into something more aloof. "I take it that's a yes?"

"I haven't gone over every inch of the house and my possessions," he said archly. "We just returned last night from Malibu, after friends notified me of this outrage. But there are several valuable pieces of my wife's jewelry missing, for starters."

"Ah," I said, aiming for a neutral tone. "A list of what's missing will help. If you do wish me to investigate the theft, that is."

"The theft *and* the thieves," Bercain corrected me. "My name is the most valuable asset under assault here."

I nodded soberly. "I understand."

"Do you know any of these Squatters, then?" he asked.

"Not personally, no. I stopped by out of curiosity last summer, when they first set up housekeeping there. I understand more people have joined them since, but I haven't been back. I can look into it if you wish."

"I *do* wish, yes," he responded, making the verb sound like a royal edict.

I reached into the bottom drawer of my desk for a copy of my standard contract and went over it with him. His manner remained distracted, however, and I doubted he took in much before he waved a square-cut hand and said, "I'm sure it's fine. Whatever others agree to."

I took *others* to include my recent bonds-bereft client and gave Bercain the same New York-standard hourly fee and advance. At this rate, I thought, I might actually be able to afford a home myself someday. I wondered idly whether such a change in my fortunes would affect my affinity for people like the Squatters. I hoped not.

"The charges on the flyer," I said, trying to find tactful wording for my question. "Do you have any idea where they might have come from? Any . . . incidents or misunderstandings?"

He rose from the client chair abruptly and began

pacing. "Who knows what twisted ideas these people have."
He glared at me again with that implication of complicity. I
saw I wasn't likely to get anywhere in this one-on-one mode;
he seemed to find it confrontational. Maybe putting the
questions in his court would make him more cooperative.

"Perhaps you could do this to help me sort it all out," I
said. "If you'd take the flyer and go down it point by point
and write down anything you can think of that could have
been misconstrued in some way to give rise to those charges."

He stopped pacing and stared at me, his eyes narrowing
with what was either appraisal or suspicion.

"It will help me know where to start," I said coolly.
"And perhaps I can work backward from there to get leads
on who these people are." My tone was one of closure. It
was my sense that I'd get more respect from this man if I
took charge of ending the interview.

I stepped toward him and extended my hand. "As
soon as you can get that to me, I'll begin the investigation
immediately."

Some, if not all, signs of doubt had faded from his face,
and he returned the handshake. "I want this done with the
utmost speed and discretion," he said, signing the contract
and a check with a flourish worthy of John Hancock.

I nodded. "Of course."

When Bercain left the office, with one last penetrating
look from the doorway, I sank into my chair, feeling
strangely drained by the encounter. I was used to a more
needy sort of client, I guessed, looking to me for strength.
This man . . . What exactly *was* he looking for? And how
close were those charges to the truth?

CHAPTER
3

WITH BERCAIN'S ADVANCE safe in the bank, giving me my first healthy balance in months, I headed out to the Squatters' encampment.

I knew there was a dirt one-lane drive to the camp off Wolf Road but decided not to come in by the front door and parked my shabby little Civic instead at the fairgrounds. Past the empty exhibition barn and the now-desolate show-rings and grandstands, there was a path beaten by the media in the early days to the new tent city.

It took some finding now, the Squatters' fifteen minutes of fame having extended only until the end of the summer. Now the path, when I located it amid the brush at the northern edge of Shepherd's Woods, was little more than two vehicle-wide rivulets of standing water, punctuated by ruts and rocks that hadn't given way to the weight of the sound trucks.

Whenever possible I like to make my first acquaintance with people under suspicion incognito. Having to be party to a direct encounter is distracting at best, and the other party is likely to be on his best behavior. So I made my way gingerly along the woodland path mostly reclaimed now by nature, carefully pinching overarching thorny vines between thumb and forefinger to bend them back out of my way, thinking that small fingers do come in handy now and then.

My feet tried to be just as nimble, hopping from root to rock in a vain attempt to keep my tennies dry. Nonetheless, by the time I made it to the crude longhouse the group had erected as their public space, I was thoroughly punctured, wet, and chilled.

My memory had served, though, from my first visit: There was one tall window on that northern wall, looking into what served as the Squatters' dining room.

The woods had nearly conquered that clearing too, so I was able to approach the longhouse under cover most of the way. My head even cleared the windowsill.

There wasn't a whole lot to see, though. Only three persons were seated on the benches of the worn picnic table, their backs slumped in postures of weariness or defeat—or both. One of the men I recognized as Denny Lockett, the spokesman for the group. His blond hair looked to have come straight off the pillow, and his rumpled plaid wool shirt and frayed jeans gave him a decidedly less dapper image than the one I remembered from the group's early months.

The other two looked no better off. The long face and lank black hair of the older man were mirrored in the adolescent boy, whose long legs were arranged awkwardly under the table's bench.

The conversation looked desultory at best, so I didn't sweat the fact that I couldn't hear it through the closed window. I watched until the older man and the boy stood up and passed out of my vision into the kitchen behind, then let the sight of the flickering fire in the woodstove lure me inside.

For a brief moment as I entered the longhouse through its front door, Denny Lockett's face remained blank; then the wattage of his golden-boy smile returned, and he stood, crossing toward me with his hand out.

"Molly, isn't it?" he said, and I was duly pleased to be remembered.

"We met last spring when I stopped by," I said. "I live in the woods south of here."

"Of course."

Broad-shouldered, of medium height, with curly blond hair atop an apparently wide-open face, Denny had appeared when I met him to be the prototypical PR man, easygoing and engaging. Now he looked older than the intervening eight months could account for but still able to tap into the "up" energy. I guessed his age at mid-twenties.

"Just in time for breakfast," he said.

I must have looked around doubtfully, because he laughed. "Well, almost."

"I'd be happy to help," I said, glancing at my watch. Nine-forty: I'd have time before I was due back in town.

"Great," he said easily. "We try to have it together by ten o'clock."

I was put to chopping onions and home-canned tomatoes for the scrambled eggs Denny cracked by the dozens into a big aluminum bowl. Feeding this many, I thought, must get pricey. I said as much.

"True," Denny said cheerfully, "but we grow as much as we can ourselves."

"Do people work? Off the place, I mean?"

"Some," he said, and set the bowl of eggs on a metal cart, returning to the industrial-size refrigerator for a small butt of ham, which he began dicing on the same deeply gashed butcher block.

Behind me, the man who had been introduced only as "Frank" slid a big pan of corn-bread batter into the gas oven. I was about to speak to him when Denny said casually, "You're a P.I., right?"

I tried to remember whether I'd told him that when I was there before. I didn't think so.

"Right," I said, as easily.

He flashed me a grin. "On duty?"

"Not necessarily," I hedged, then changed my mind. "Actually, I've been hired by Edmond Bercain to find out who's behind those WANTED posters in town. He thinks it might be you people."

If I'd hoped for surprise to disarm Denny's reaction, I was not rewarded. He grinned. "So Mr. Bercain has heard of poor-little-us?"

I shrugged. "Enough to make him suspicious, I guess."

"Ah. And you? Are you suspicious?"

"My professional mind is always open," I said, and left it at that.

I had hoped to get a chance to speak to Frank before the others arrived. He had been the oldest of the group when I'd visited before. But his lanky body drew near only long enough to take the corn bread out of the oven and for me to say, "How are you liking it here?"

"I keep busy" was the short reply, and he was gone.

As for the boy I took to be his son, he shambled about doing the tasks his father ordered, but only after the second or third repetition. Mostly he seemed intent on his feet, though he did flick a look my way from time to time.

Then the others came straggling in, hanging their coats on a row of hooks screwed into the board-and-batten wall, and I ferried back and forth putting food and plates on the table while they eyed me with mild curiosity.

I recognized a few of them, but no names, so was glad Denny introduced them all as we seated ourselves at the long table. Only first names, but I made mental notes; my memory for names is not my strongest suit.

A tall young woman named Iris settled on the bench to my left, while the boy, now identified as Leonard, was directed to my right. Denny sat at the end of the table, in an armchair that made me think of Daddy Bear, and Dorothy, a plain middle-aged woman, sat at the other end, on an armless Mama Bear chair.

Across from me, a big-bellied man called Sam, with a black-and-white beard, made the table shake as he pulled the bench up to it—after which an intelligent-looking young woman introduced as Maia made him stand up and pulled the bench back out to move inside herself, drawing the bench smoothly up to the table again.

We had already passed the dishes and filled our plates before the last to arrive appeared, a striking but sullen-looking girl with big hair whose age I guessed at sixteen or seventeen. She sat to Dorothy's right, and the older woman gave her a disapproving motherly glare.

"So how's it going?" I asked the table at large, with my friendliest smile.

There were mumblings around forkfuls of food, little eye contact.

"Fine," Dorothy said firmly.

"If you like cold and wet," grumbled the teenager.

There was general silence.

I tried focusing on my nearest neighbor, whose height seemed to be mostly in her legs, since her head was not that much higher than mine.

"Have you been here long?" I asked her.

" 'Bout six months."

"How's it going?"

"Hard."

This was a woman of few words; I figured I might as well make them meaningful. "Did you lose your place?"

She cast a sidelong glance at me, as though the question was a rude one. Which it pretty much was. "If you don't mind my asking," I added.

"Taxes kept going up till we couldn't pay."

There was a silence, which I let rest. Then she added, "I

wanted a second mortgage. That little farm was all I ever had. But Carl said no, he was goin' to a commune, get away from all this greed."

I noticed Denny watching us from the end of the table.

"And did he?" I said. "Go to a commune?"

"Yeah. Someplace in Virginia."

I'd placed her accent as more like Tennessee, accents being a necessary skill for actresses, which I used to be.

"And you didn't want to go?"

"I had enough of the South."

"So he's still there?"

"Last I heard. I guess he likes it." She turned toward me then and almost smiled. "Looks like I ended up in a commune anyhow, sort of."

"You seen one commune, you seen 'em all," Sam said, his blue eyes almost disappearing into laugh lines.

"You've been in communes?" I asked.

"A few."

"How does this one compare?"

"This is not a commune," Dorothy stated, in a tone that suggested she wouldn't be caught dead in one.

Her daughter rolled her eyes.

"Do you work outside as well?" I asked of the table in general.

"I do," Iris said. "Part-time, at the diner."

"Our intent generally is more political than economic," Denny said.

"Speak for yourself," Maia snapped. "Some of us just have nowhere else to go."

"Molly is a private investigator," Denny said then, in a somewhat louder voice. "She's working for Mr. Bercain."

There was a sudden freeze on the conversation, but Maia's gaze from behind her rimless glasses fixed on mine. "Really?" she said coldly. "Have you worked for him long?"

"He just hired me this morning. To find out who was behind the WANTED posters."

No one asked what WANTED posters.

Maia speared a piece of ham and a diced tomato and bit them off her fork like a snapping turtle.

"Edmond Bercain," she said, when she had dispatched her mouthful, "is not a nice man."

I held my tongue, hoping she would go on. But Denny cut in first. "Maia had quite a successful business, before—"

Maia turned and stopped him with a look. "The man is without morals," she said to me simply.

"Maia's big on morality," Denny interjected again.

"Somebody has to be," she snapped back.

I waited with baited breath, hoping their debate would continue, but it was not to be. At that moment Leonard said to my right shoulder, "Are you really one of those private-eye guys?"

I turned with irritation but was disarmed by his ingenuous smile. "Yes," I said, "I am."

But as I turned back toward Maia, he spoke up again. "You're not a man."

"I've noticed that," I said. "Luckily, I don't have to be."

His glowing face wouldn't let me turn away again. "You got a gun?"

"Not here."

"I do!" he said triumphantly.

"Don't talk foolishness," his father snapped.

Leonard cringed a little, his eyes downcast. "Do too," he mumbled.

Dorothy stood abruptly. "Anybody want fruit? There are apples in the cold cellar."

As though on cue, everybody at the table stood.

"I'd like to talk to you further," I said as Maia began putting on the jacket she'd kept on her lap.

Her mouth twisted in a wry smile. "I wouldn't want to disillusion you about your new client," she said, and turned and strode out the door.

CHAPTER
4

I GOT BACK TO TOWN just in time to change into dry clothes and get to the middle school for the work session I was supposed to supervise, making luminarias for the Saints and Sinners Parade that night.

Since streetlights exist on only the four-block stretch of nighttime commercial activity in Grace, the more extensive route of the parade needed additional lighting. Having borrowed its parade style from New Orleans, the organizers cast about for lighting ideas and settled on the practice by Southwest missions of using candles sheathed in luminous paper to light the way of religious processions. The word apparently had gotten around that I'd been a theater major in college, so it was assumed that I would know how to construct such staging arts. I said I hadn't the least clue but agreed to give it a shot.

My workforce was to be a bunch of kids declared "at risk" by the school's powers that be. At risk for what was unclear, but for whatever reason the youngsters, teen and preteen, were felt to be performing in school at less than their best and might be on their way to more serious violations of acceptable behavior. So they became my crew in the crafting of candle shields.

The youths, they said, would be a handful and wouldn't

want to do anything constructive, but I didn't really find that to be the case. Having been a bit of a handful myself in those years (not to mention since), I found their angst a reasonable response to raging hormones and a deeply flawed world. I figured that their boredom at being penned in a room doing nothing all afternoon would serve to interest them in the project eventually.

Some got involved faster than others. The boy I'd been told would give me the most trouble—one Mikah Horn, age fifteen—turned out to be the most gifted artist and a helpful assistant. The boy's straight black hair and dark eyes beneath heavy brows contributed to the sullen look obligatory for his age: half disdain, half insecurity. They were not trusting eyes, but reachable, I hoped. Give him enough room and he'd come around. And he did.

As did his sidekick, his little sister Emily, age two. Their mother, I'd been told, seemed to be gone much of the time, so it had fallen to Mikah to look after his sister, and he never let her out of his sight.

Nor vice versa. Emily was not without her own symptoms of trouble. Clearly bright—precocious even—the child did not seem to feel the need to communicate with anyone. Through language at least. Her concentration on what she herself was doing apparently left no room for the distraction of conversation. But she kept a sharp eye on her brother and followed his lead.

I told the kids what was needed and that I had no idea how to get there from here (not much of an exaggeration), so those with any interest at all were left to improvise. Mikah got there first, devising a way to make a sheath of the material that would stand up around the candle without collapsing into it. Then Emily got busy with the colored chalk I'd given her, covering each sheet with a child's slanting scribble, but in a sequence of colors that seemed far from random. On one she used yellow, bleeding to orange, then red, while on another a vivid blue was overlaid with green, producing a shimmering effect that, when backlit by the candle, seemed to capture the ever-shifting colors of the sea.

Their activity was contagious, and soon others followed suit, producing candle coverings according to their own lights. Some of the "lights" seemed decidedly brighter than others to my eye, but I tried to stifle my natural bent toward quality control and let the creators create as they would.

Mikah then moved on to further innovation, experimenting with poking holes in the paper with the point of a pen, creating designs that the candle, when lit, projected into the darkness. He said he thought he'd seen it somewhere, and he probably had, but I was impressed.

The other kids especially liked the puncturing part, and the resulting shields were nothing if not original. One particularly hostile boy named Jason Floss put his extensive knowledge of comic-book language to use and was turning out luminarias projecting *ZAP!* and *SHA-BAM!* like an assembly lineman on acid.

By the time the group's attention lagged, we had enough lanterns to mark not only the designated route along Parsley, down Sunflower, up Rose, and across Persimmon, but could continue through the shops behind Parsley, up Dandelion to Daisy, and back across Nutmeg, all the way to Chamomile. I cannot report that Mayor Stephenson-Roth and the honorable Hugh Gidoux, when they arrived, were exactly thrilled with our products, but drawing them aside, I reminded them of the human aspect of the project's goals, and they agreed to use everybody's works of art, no matter how dubious.

By the time the kids and I had finished setting them up along the parade route, the first busload of participants was just arriving, and it was clear I wouldn't have a chance to costume myself.

It was just as well. I had considered rerunning my French maid impersonation, which had amused Simon and his guests at a whodunit party at his home the year before. But that seemed, in both senses, an inside joke. After a chilly morning, the afternoon had been sunny and downright balmy for December, but the unaccustomed sun had set, and the temperature felt inhospitable to low-cut necklines, miniskirts, and mesh stockings.

Besides, without Gray, my significant other, to stimulate to some end, what really was the point? New Year's Eve for Timothy Gray, chief of police of Emerald on the mainland, is one of the most demanding holidays. Add liquor and a spirit of year-end abandon to the standard craziness of the driving populace, and you've got your hands full.

This pedestrian parade crowd, though, seemed in a lighthearted mood and had gone all out on costumes. I positioned myself atop a reinstated outdoor table at the Pirates' Cove Restaurant on Parsley and watched a tipsy ballerina trip over her toe shoes into a whiskey tub of decorative cabbage; a Frankenstein's monster with an actual zipper at his temple holding hands with a chap whose mild Dr. Jekyll mask on one side of his face warred with a brutish Mr. Hyde on the other; and an organ grinder with an oversize monkey who, in a confusion of fairy tales, was leading a pack of small gray rats into the All-Scream Ice Cream Shoppe. Even Edvard Munch's painting "The Scream" was represented by a chalk-white face in that twisting, agonized expression, over a humped black cape. As I said, it's an artsy town.

The parade was not to begin until eleven o'clock, to allow time for those from the West Island to get there by bus, since Grace's parking is limited and the island's free buses were seen as a safer way for people to be transported on that revelers' night. But by ten, Parsley Street was crammed with costumed celebrants and more were pressing in from the Primrose bus stop and the King's Castle resort to the west. By ten-thirty they had to let those nearest Sunflower begin to move, just to accommodate the newcomers.

For that Mardi Gras flavor, an assortment of musicians

had been positioned along the parade route with instructions to simulate a Dixieland sound, and by moving time everybody was into the swing of it. The trio posted nearest me—a trumpet, a trombone, and a kettle drum—broke into "When the Saints Go Marching In," and by the fifth chorus whole new waves of celebrants were passing by.

I had worked up a sweat, clapping my hands and stamping my feet in my version of a Creole jig, when a high keening sound, somehow shriller than the others, carried to me on the clear night air. It made me shiver in my windbreaker. I glanced at my digital watch—12:02—and that seemed to explain it: the old year shrieking out as the new was ushered in. I thought no more about it until I was roused from my camper bed some five hours later by Chief Belgium, who advised me that my client, Edmond Anderson Bercain, was dead, and the M.E.'s estimate was midnight.

CHAPTER
5

"WHAT?" I SAID for the third or fourth time, standing in the doorway of my camper, blinking into the twin suns of the headlights Chief Belgium had left on along with the running motor.

The chief didn't bother to repeat his news again. "Bercain hired you, right? Did you see him at all last night?" His voice was even more impatient than usual. Chief Belgium had moved to the island after fifteen years on the L.A. force and had considered it at least semiretirement.

"No," I said, running my fingers through the sleep-flattened hair at my left temple. "Unless he was in costume."

"You'd better get dressed and come to the station, tell me what you know," Belgium said wearily. After years of relative peace and quiet, this made the third murder on the East Island in a year, and I had been connected to the other two as well. The man's tone suggested that he held me at least partially responsible.

"Where was the scene?" I asked, still trying to get a handle on this turn of events.

"Daisy," he said, the word sounding silly in his harsh voice. "Just below Bay. M.E. thinks about midnight," he added, anticipating my next question.

"The parade wouldn't have gone that far," I said,

surprised that my brain was working at all in its sleep-disrupted state.

"Must be why nobody claims to have seen the crime," Belgium said dryly, turning back to his squad car. "Make it quick. I've got lots of questions."

Unfortunately, I had very few answers. Ten minutes into his questioning I was already repeating myself. "He just said he wanted to know who was behind the WANTED posters."

"He have any guesses?"

"The Squatters. Though it didn't seem more than a suspicion. If he had any reason to believe the group was involved, he didn't tell me."

"He know any of that crew?"

"Not that he said. I think that's one of the reasons he hired me."

"So you know them?"

"Not really."

"That a yes or a no?"

I sighed. "I stopped by once last spring, when they first set up housekeeping. But I didn't stay long, and I've had no contact with any of them since. Until yesterday. I went over there right after he hired me yesterday morning."

"And?"

"And my guess would be that they might have had something to do with the posters. But murder . . ." I thought of the intensity of Maia's hazel-green eyes, magnified by her thick glasses. "I'd have to probe further."

"So do it," Belgium said, heaving his weight out of his desk chair. "Better you than us probably, first off. But make it quick; we need to move on this."

I nodded. "Do I tell them? About the murder?"

Belgium thought a minute. "Use your judgment. If you think it might trigger a reaction . . . We'll be right behind you anyway." He checked his watch. "We'll figure to show up there around eight, eight-thirty." He moved to grab his jacket from the coat tree by the door and shouldered it on.

I stood. "You haven't said how Bercain was killed."

"No." Belgium's high forehead, under its thatch of near-white hair, furrowed in thought, his pale gray eyes distracted. Then he said, "Coroner's not through with the body yet."

"But . . ."

"Your basic blunt instrument. Enough to cave in his skull; must have been a lot of strength behind it."

"Or anger."

"Or both. Take your gun."

As I followed him through the mostly empty outer office toward the street, I thought probably I should be flattered, being put in the front line of the troops this way. But more likely, Belgium, like Bercain, just saw me as one of the woodland folk, only slightly more reliable in my allegiance.

This time I circled the encampment through the woods and approached from the rear, behind the line of tents at the back edge of their clearing. It was a little after six; I wanted to see if everybody was there and accounted for.

Of course, I didn't know whose tent was whose or when an occupant might have arrived. If someone was absent, that wouldn't in itself be proof of anything. Ditto being present. But it was a place to start.

There were six tents visible and a tepee. That left somebody unhoused. Unless Leonard or the teenager bunked with his or her parent.

I settled myself on the driest surface I could find: one of the umpteen trees blown down in last month's windstorm.

I hadn't long to wait. From a green tent—the newest-looking, though its wet canvas sagged as much as the others—Dorothy's figure emerged, wearing a plastic rain cape over gray sweats and carrying a dark navy towel. She stood indecisively for a moment, looking to her right at nothing I could see from where I sat, then headed slowly in that direction.

It wasn't until she parted a clump of ferns between two hemlocks that I saw a sliver of red. The seventh tent? The daughter's?

The woman's efforts at stealth made me suspect that she was checking up on her daughter's presence, the same as I was. Or maybe the number of occupants in her tent. In any case, she soon emerged from the site and shuffled in sockless sneakers to the back of the longhouse and entered by its rear kitchen door, her shoulders slumped in a posture of depression.

The next to appear was Sam, from the tepee several tents down. He headed for the nearest bushes, staggering a bit, though whether from semisleep or the aftereffects of drugs or booze I couldn't be sure.

He stood there long enough for a marathon pee and was returning to his lair, fumbling with his pants, when it occurred to me that he might now be more useful to me as a consultant than a suspect. So I hustled from my hiding place to the worn dirt path that ran the length of the tents and hailed him as though I'd just come around the corner of the longhouse.

He stopped, staring at me as though he hadn't the least idea who I was.

" 'Morning," I said. "I'm looking for Denny. Which is his tent?"

It seemed to take him a while to focus on the question. Then he said, "He's not in it. Stayed in town last night."

"Ah," I said. "Does he do that often?"

"From time to time." His brain was waking up. "Something you need from him?"

"Nothing urgent," I said. "I was just going by on my run and thought I'd stop and see—"

It was as far as I got. A shot rang out from the tent behind me, sending me two feet into the air and landing with my gun drawn.

Sam had almost no reaction at all. "Leonard," he said calmly. "Leonard and his plane collection. Fancies himself a fighter pilot."

Then Frank lunged from the tent beyond, swearing as he ran. He disappeared into his son's tent, already shouting, "Dammit, boy, how the hell did you find that ammunition? Don't you have any sense at all? Every shot you fire at those planes goes right through the tent. It's a wonder you haven't drowned by now. And what if somebody was passing by? This is the last time—"

Sam looked at the gun in my hand without interest and yawned widely. "Any message you want to leave for Denny?"

"No," I said. "I'll catch him later."

I'd have liked to know the whereabouts of Maia before I left, but I had to make good on my story. Nobody appeared from any of the other tents; apparently Leonard's shooting sprees were old hat. I'd let Belgium take care of that one. News delivery of the killing too: If I was going to continue my investigation here, I'd probably find out more in the long run if I were as little identified with the police as possible.

As to continuing the investigation, I thought the next order of business should be contact with my client's widow, to see whether she wanted me to pursue the matter of the flyers. I'd put in a call to her from my office, find out when she'd feel up to seeing me.

I had a stop to make first, though. Retrieving my car from the Wolf Road entrance to the Squatters' drive, I headed back to town, leaving a brief report for Belgium at the station via my new cell phone.

I followed Wolf until it became Bay Road at the Greater Grace limits, then cruised down that western edge of downtown Grace to Daisy. A light rain, little more than a mist, had begun, though dark clouds to the north threatened more. I pulled into the senior center's parking lot at Bay and Daisy.

There was a small crowd—mostly of seniors—still gathered outside the yellow crime-scene tape, which described a rectangle the width of the street and about twelve feet long. Detective Hart Burrows was still posted at the scene, but all the evidence-gathering appeared to be finished. I caught Burrows's eye, then ducked under the tape to get closer.

There wasn't much to see. They still make chalk outlines of bodies in Grace, and the misting rain hadn't begun to obliterate this one yet. The body apparently had sprawled facedown, indicating a blow to the back of the head. Only a small smear of blood was visible to the right of where the head had fallen facing left.

"This all there is?" I asked Burrows.

He nodded. "No fingerprints we could find on anything."

"Shoe prints?"

"Nothing useful. It had to be dry last night. You on the case?"

"Not really. Bercain hired me yesterday to look into the posters thing."

"Short job."

"Seems that way."

I circled the outline again, then nodded my thanks and ducked back under the tape and continued down Daisy toward Dandelion.

I wasn't looking for anything in particular. Many people must have passed this way between midnight and the current 7:50 A.M. But I walked slowly, studying both sides of the sidewalk, until I reached People's Park—or what was left of it after a fire there the summer before. All of the play equipment had been handcrafted of handpainted wood, true to the P.C. code of Grace, so there was little left. Only the iron base, spokes, and railing remained of a push-powered revolving ride at the park's center, so I headed for it.

A rubble of ashes was all that was left of the wood, rained on and mixed with mud over the past months into a black mulch.

I bent over the area, saw a few slight edges of leftover shoe prints facing left—the direction anyone pushing the ride would have been facing—and one set of clearer toe prints, somewhat larger than a child's, facing the rail.

There was also a sliver of something lighter than the dirt, which I reached to pick up. Nearly a foot-long jagged piece of wood, maybe splintered from something larger, it was bone-dry, as only age or hot sun could have made it. It was probably nothing, but I slid it into the pocket of my yellow rain slicker and headed back to the office.

CHAPTER
6

I DIDN'T HAVE TO CALL Mrs. Bercain; she called me. The light was blinking when I entered my office, and hers was the second message.

The voice was calm and clear. "This is Kendall Bercain, Ms. Piper. I understand my husband hired you yesterday. I would like to speak to you, please."

She had said "yesterday," so the message couldn't have been left before her husband was killed. I returned the call.

I was put right through by a woman with a Latina accent.

"Thank you for returning my call, Ms. Piper. I wonder if you might be available to come see me this morning." The voice was just as cool.

"Yes, of course," I said.

"Would now be convenient for you?"

"Yes," I said again.

From the directions she gave me, I surmised that the Bercain home was situated—no great surprise—on Bread-loaf Hill, from whence came most paychecks in Grace. Those of the hourly wage, in fact, called it Bread-and-Butter Hill, reflecting their economic reality. The true name came from its shape, rising on the southern crest of Grace, its backside sloping into Shepherd's Woods.

The Bercain home was near the top, the long driveway at 651 Temple winding up a poplar-flanked slope until, all at once, the house was there before you. Pretty much a standard ranch but surrounded by beautifully balanced landscaping of evergreens, dormant perennials, and ornamental grasses.

I hated to ruin the effect with my unsightly little '82 Honda Civic, so I stopped, uncertain where to park. There was a separate garage, so I pulled around to its far side and left her there.

The doorway was framed by two large concrete pots, so heavy they had to be permanent, though their contents probably changed with the seasons. At present they held about all that was blooming: twin groupings of soft pink Helleborus—the "Christmas rose"—surrounded by gray lamb's ears. Not actually a rose, the Helleborus's resemblance triggered my natural instinct to stoop and smell, until the door opened and I quickly straightened.

I don't know what I expected Kendall Bercain to look like, but it would have been far from the woman who opened the door. I took her, in fact, for the housekeeper.

Apparently it had happened before, because the make-upless, big-boned woman in denim, her straight black hair chopped off at the shoulders, stuck out her hand and said, "I'm Kendall," before I'd even had time to identify myself.

She, on the other hand, displayed no surprise at the unlikely looks of my person for my line of work. But maybe she'd already seen or heard of me, my being the only P.I. on the island. I didn't attend most social functions and wriggled out ASAP of those I did, but it was a small town and word got around.

She ushered me from the entrance hall, with its dizzying pattern of black-and-white tiles, into one of those designer living rooms with dark green walls and busy floral drapes and carpet. Already I was feeling claustrophobic, so I was relieved that we passed through it into a wide-open room glassed on three sides.

I stopped, taking in the long, smooth undulations of the backyard, a study in shapes and textures and the infinite shades of green and brown. Curving beds outlined with gray river rocks snaked down to a wooden arch, through which a bark path led to parts unseen.

"This is really beautiful," I said. "Are you the artist?"

It was the only smile I would see from her that day, but it lit her face in wonderful ways.

I took the seat she gestured me toward, on a wicker chair with a plump green pillow. "I appreciate your seeing me, so soon after your husband's . . . death," I said.

"On the contrary. I knew he'd hired you about that WANTED poster thing." The left corner of her mouth twitched as though tempted by another smile. "But I'd like to retain you for my own investigation. Of his murder."

She stood, turning toward the blue-green mist of the backyard. "I didn't do it, you see. And isn't it always the spouse that's suspected? I'd like you to look elsewhere, if for no other reason than to clear me."

My surprise at her candor must have shown, because she said, "Not quite the grieving widow, am I? I had come to detest my husband. Behind that public charm was . . . well, quite another person."

She didn't seem inclined to elaborate, so I went back to square one. "I brought his contract with me. I thought maybe you'd want to cancel. But you could sign it too, I guess, if you want me to proceed. I have his advance already."

"Fine," she said, and reached for it, along with the pen I fished out of my bag.

"It was the poster's attack on his name that seemed to bother him most," I said. "More than the thefts."

"His name," she scoffed. Then her face stiffened.

"He suspected the Squatters group of being behind the posters."

"I don't care about the posters," she said briskly. "And I seriously doubt that anyone in that bunch killed him, so I'd like you to look elsewhere there too."

I was becoming uneasy, particularly after the hostility I'd seen at the Squatters' camp. "You're not asking me to limit my investigation, are you?" I asked carefully.

She made a dismissive gesture with her ringless left hand. "Go wherever it sends you, by all means. But I suspect that my husband"—she pronounced the word with a contemptuous twist—"ruffled more feathers than theirs. I want you to look into every area of his life. Business *and* pleasure." The last word got a twist as well.

Then she moved toward the door through which we'd come, the interview apparently over. I had a headful of questions, but I stood reluctantly. Maybe this was all she was ready for at this point. I'd set up a meeting later, when I'd done a little more homework myself.

I remember thinking, as we soberly shook hands at the door, that Kendall Bercain had issued me a challenge of sorts and I was being sent off to solve the puzzle. It crossed my mind that she might already have some of those pieces herself.

Which only added to the bemusement I felt when the first of the "clues" was lying on the floor of my office when I returned to it after a fortifying brunch at The Blue Heron.

Apparently it had been slid under the door, and I noticed it only when I turned back to hang up my coat. It was in a plain white business envelope, the sort you can pick up in boxes of fifty at any supermarket or discount store, lined with a crosshatched pattern to qualify as "security" against prying eyes.

The paper inside was equally nondescript, plain 8½-by-11-inch typing paper. But the three words stuck to it were colorful enough, and so big they nearly covered the page: TRUTH IN ADVERTISING. Each letter was a different size, style, and color—cut, it appeared, from a glossy magazine. The message was so ornate and artfully done, it seemed more a playful than a surreptitious act.

So what was it? My client's sly way of telling me that the poster charges were true? Or signposts to those whose "feathers" he "ruffled"?

Or a message from the poster of the posters? The Squatters, one or more? Or someone(s) not even considered yet? I was torn between sort of enjoying the game of it and feeling frustrated that if someone had something to tell me, why not just come out and say it? This was not a mystery party, after all; someone had been murdered.

I took my messages off the machine, returned a call, then hopped down the stairway to the law office of my friend Eugene Mulholland, who occupies the ground-floor office in my building.

"Got a minute?" I asked after his "Come in."

He turned in his swivel chair and leaned back, stretching his arms and flexing his shoulders, as though both had been held motionless for hours.

Which might have been the case. In the year and a half since I'd set up shop in this little half-restored Victorian, I hadn't been able to find a pattern to the hours Eugene spent in his office. He might be there at dawn when I came in to place a call to the East Coast, or after dark if I dropped by to pick up my messages. Or I might not see him for days.

"I've got a quick question."

"Take your time," he said easily. "I could use the break."

"Have you ever met Kendall Bercain?"

"Mmm. I've seen her occasionally, at requisite functions. Can't really say I've *met* her, though. She was always pretty much off to the sidelines. Didn't look very approachable."

"She's a client now," I said, "since her husband's

murder. He had just hired me to look into the WANTED poster thing."

"I thought I saw him coming out of the building yesterday. Did he take the posters that seriously? As a threat?"

I shrugged. "He was definitely agitated. But he seemed more concerned about his reputation than his life."

Eugene grinned. "That's a politician for you." He stood up to pace, and I sat on the edge of his desk, watching him. "I'd be surprised," he said, "if that was the first time anybody'd sullied his name."

"Oh? Do you know something I should?"

"Just an impression. The man always seemed to be trying too hard. As though he had something to prove. I don't know his background, but my bet would be blue-collar. Self-made man and all that. The vocabulary, the enunciation—they always sounded self-conscious, too perfect not to be deliberately learned."

"And his wife?"

"Oh, she looked like she'd given up proving anything to anybody long ago. She just wanted to get back home and into her jeans."

I had come to value Eugene's appraisals of people. It's what gave him the edge over an opposing attorney, I suspected, upping his win-to-lose ratio.

"So you saw her as indifferent? Retiring? Antisocial?"

"Maybe all of the above. But, remember, I hardly saw her at all beyond fleeting glimpses."

I went back up to my office and placed a call to my new client, wife of my former client, now deceased. I'd hoped this relationship would be longer-lived, but if she was playing games with me . . .

The voice that answered at the Bercain residence was thickly Hispanic. She told me to wait, she would see if "*la señora* want to speak." She came back shortly to inform me that she did not. Not that she was out, just "no want to speak." I decided there was no use pressing the point and left my name with a request that *"la señora"* return my call.

I leaned back in my swivel desk chair, in my thinking position, rocked back and forth, then took a few spins. At the farthest backward tilt my feet don't touch the floor, so I propel my twirls by tapping the knob on the top drawer with my toe and giving myself a push. The rules are, if I miss it, I can't use anything else and have to let the momentum die down.

So what were the rules for this case? If I suspected my client of playing games with me, did I have to confront her before continuing the investigation? Should I treat this "clue" as something to be explored or as a diversion? TRUTH IN ADVERTISING. If the truth lay in something "advertised," presumably that put it in the public domain, something out there that either had been made known to me already or that I could easily access.

I snagged my rain slicker from the hook on the door and headed for the offices of the *Grace Guardian* five blocks away on Nutmeg and Rhododendron. I would be checking its files anyway; might as well be sooner than later.

I found Bernie Wu, the paper's photographer, at his desk, looking dejected.

"Glad I caught you!" I said, a bit breathless from having run all the way. (I figure if I run everywhere instead of walk, I earn a thousand extra calories a day. And I eat every one of them.)

"I wondered when you were going to come to your senses," Bernie said, perking up. "I keep telling you we were meant for each other."

Bernie thinks the fact that we are both under five feet is

a message from the gods to throw ourselves into each other's arms.

I ignored the remark. "You know what I want. Were you out last night? Did you get any shots of the Daisy area around midnight when they think he was killed?" (You don't have to identify a victim; there isn't even a murder a year on the whole island. Except those under my nose last year, that is.)

"Too late, babe, the police already took the film. From the entire night." He frowned. "There was some great stuff in there too. That parade was bitchin'."

I was disappointed but not surprised. I wasn't the only one working the room, as it were.

"Did they say how long they'd keep it?" But I knew the answer to that too; Belgium would never commit himself to a timetable where evidence was concerned.

"I was about to go over there—*again*," Bernie said. "See if they'd at least give me back some of the clearly irrelevant shots of the parade. At least enough for a full-page insert. They could keep copies."

"Lots of luck," I said.

His expression told me he wasn't betting the farm on it either. "With the murder now too," he said wistfully, "people are going to be snatching up this issue like it was gold. Mike did an extra run this morning."

He sighed. I sighed. Then we went our separate ways.

For the past year the paper had been modernizing its morgue, from stacks for each year in the basement to access only on microfilm. This was not a popular move with me. There is something very concretely satisfying about poring over old newsprint in a basement smelling of aging paper and printer's ink, sure that the very next page will have just the item you're looking for.

I cannot say the same for plastic film. Most of my

energy seems to go into just getting the bloody machine to work and the lens to focus. And if you do succeed in cranking that slick plastic strip straight under your nose, just squinting at its glary type through those mammoth goggles probably takes years off your sight. I wondered if I could claim it as workmen's comp when I could no longer ply my trade. After a couple of fruitless hours, I gave it up for the day.

CHAPTER
7

I woke the next morning to the sound of heavy rain pelting the metal top of my camper. The direct route to a bad mood: My running trail in the woods would be mud, impassable.

On the way into my office I stopped at the Spotted Owl Café on Wolf Road, thinking a good hearty breakfast might cheer me up. But they were out of blintzes and my eggs were hard.

There is a point in an island winter when, if the rain keeps beating out the sun by more than four to one, everybody goes into a slump. My slump seemed to be shared by the other breakfasters at the Spotted Owl, and solemn photos of its nearly extinct namesake on every wall didn't help.

I parked only four doors up on Dahlia, but my hair was still a wet tumbleweed by the time I unlocked the front door. I trudged up the stairs to my office, almost glad to hear the zither music that accompanies the morning meditations of T-om, the building's resident mystic. The zither's sharp wail usually affects me like a fingernail across a blackboard, but any medium of spirituality was welcome on such a morning.

Ask folks why they live on Prince Island, and at least three out of four will give you some element of spirituality in their answers. Maybe it's the presence of some of the last old-growth forest in the country. Maybe it has something to do with the ratio of fertile fields to pavement. Or maybe it is simply the experience of being held in the palm of the ocean. Whatever, it gets to us all, making city maladies like ulcers and road rage almost nonexistent.

I realized when I opened my office door and saw the white envelope on the floor that, in some part of my mind, I had been anticipating it. Not with pleasure but with a certain degree of curiosity.

I picked it up with a tissue this time, in case its sender was so careless as to leave prints. The plain envelope and paper were the same, the boldness of the vivid letters: TWISTED TIMES.

Cutout letters on paper. Big deal, I told myself. So why was it feeling like such a pronouncement, a verdict?

So much for spirituality on an insulated island, I thought, and laid the thing on my desk, locked the door, and ran down the stairs, out into the rain again. Could I get any wetter than I was? Might as well be where wet was at home.

I ran down Dahlia, across Nutmeg, down Lily, and north along Lilac to Parsley, descended the switchback of mossy wooden steps too fast for safety, past the PROCEED AT YOUR OWN RISK sign, down the concrete steps to the beach, and turned right toward The Faces.

I was amazed to see that I was not alone on my soggy visit. A short, stocky form sat on a rock before them and had not turned as I dropped to the sand.

I halted, not wishing to disturb this fellow seeker. But when his contemplation seemed unbroken, I walked slowly forward and behind the figure to take a seat on my favorite rock just beyond his.

He turned then, and I was startled to see that it was the boy from the luminarias project.

"Hi, Mikah," I said.

He nodded and turned back to the wall.

The silence continued for some time, as I looked from one to another of the carved faces, their expressions changed only by the working of the sea's salt on the gray rock. Once again I was surprised at how much the same they had been created by the carver's hand yet how different each now appeared. Environment over heredity?

It was Mikah who finally broke the silence. Without turning he said, "My father was Indian."

I waited for him to say more, but he didn't, so I asked, "*Was?* Is he dead?"

"Sort of," Mikah said. Then in a moment, "He's in jail. In prison."

"Ah."

The light made a smooth sheen of the boy's wet black hair, sculpting his features in profile, still as stone.

"Do you see him?" I asked.

"No. My mother won't let me." Still he didn't turn.

"Is it close, the prison?"

"Shelton."

"On the peninsula."

"I could do it," he said, turning. "I'm fifteen! I could go on the bus."

I doubted that there was a bus down the Olympic Peninsula, but I let it pass. "Maybe she needs you at home," I said, wondering why I was taking his mother's part; I didn't even know her. Adults vs. kids?

"She just wants me to take care of Emily. *She* sure doesn't!"

"I've seen how well you do that," I said, "and how much Emily relies on you. Loves you."

"We don't have the same father," Mikah said heatedly. "But I guess that's obvious."

I remembered being told there was no man in the home. "Is he around, Emily's father? Does he see her?"

Mikah made a harsh sound. "Never. Not once." Then

after a sullen pause, "My mother said she didn't even know who he was. 'Just another asshole,' she said."

Abruptly, Mikah hoisted the sodden backpack that had been leaning against the rock and headed back toward the steps. "See ya," he said without turning.

"See ya," I called.

The encounter hadn't exactly lifted my mood, but I stood as well. I had a case to solve, and I couldn't count on The Faces to solve it for me.

When I got back to the office, I picked up the phone before even changing into dry clothes. There was a certain voice I needed to hear.

"Hi, Jeff," I said to the officer who answered. "Is he in?"

Jeff must have passed on the call without identifying the caller, because the familiar voice that answered said simply, "Gray."

"Hey, Gray," I said, and the voice warmed.

"Sweetheart!"

Only lately had he been calling me "sweetheart." Instead of the usual "babe." It puzzled me a little. But then, there were a lot of things that puzzled me about Gray lately.

"I miss you," I said.

"Me too."

"So when can I come see you?"

"The door's always open."

"But when will you be behind it?"

"Barring an outbreak of crime, any time you say."

"Tonight?"

"Tonight'd be great."

"I'll bring dinner."

"I can provide."

"That I know; why do you think I'm coming?"

An uncomfortable silence. Then, "It will be good to see you."

"Okay," I said. "About seven?"

"Great."

When I hung up there were tears in my eyes. What was going on? My relationship with Timothy Gray, first of the Chicago police force, now chief of police in Emerald, had been sexually passionate from the beginning. And it had kept that head of steam undiminished until about two months ago. Now he seemed to be distancing himself from me. As though the twelve-year difference in our ages was suddenly important. Or . . . I didn't know what.

Another woman? I couldn't believe that. I was only the second woman Gray had ever been with. He'd married his childhood sweetheart and was devoted to her until her murder, some six years before I met him. That's when he switched from prelaw to the front lines of the police academy.

We had sort of rescued each other. I had been raped and had pretty much shut down to the rest of the world. Our coming together was nothing either of us had imagined, let alone planned, but when it happened it brought us both back to the land of the living.

But lately, though we still got together most every weekend, he seemed distracted, remote, and had stopped raising the subject of marriage. I'd been in no hurry for the domestic life, though I could see it at some point in our future. But now . . . It made me uneasy.

I spent the rest of the day trying to track Carolyn Fishkorn's missing husband by calling his usual haunts in Seattle, where he'd taken off to the last two times he'd left her. The angry voice of his last girlfriend made me believe her when she told me she hadn't seen him. "And if I never do again, it will be too soon."

The branch offices of his brokerage firm up and down the West Coast claimed not to have heard from him either, asked me to let them know if I found him. It wasn't the first time I'd contacted them as myself, so just for good measure I called a buddy of his at the L.A. office, posing as Mary Lou

LeClair, telling him "Chuck" Fishkorn had given him as someone to call in case I wasn't able to reach Chuck at his office.

"I just wanted to know, you know, how these things—these 'futures' he wanted me to invest in—are going? This is the first time I ever did anything like this, you know?"

Any friend of Chuck's might have suspected that that wasn't the only thing she had done for the first time with old Chucky.

"My husband, you know, will just be awful mad if he finds out I spent my household allowance on something called 'futures.' "

But Artie Foust claimed not to have a clue where Fishkorn was either.

In frustration I called my client to give her a verbal report on my nonprogress and was ticked when she hemmed and hawed, finally saying he had "made contact" with her and told her he was "in trouble," needed her to send money to a certain post-office box to "tide him over" until he could "straighten it all out."

So was she sending him the money?

"Of course. He needs me."

Of course. I scrawled *Hopeless* across the folder and filed it in my *Hold for Foreseeable Future* file, assuaging my completion compulsion that all my investigative energies could now be turned to the Bercain case. He, at least, was one lout who could not get taken back.

CHAPTER
8

THE YELLOW-SLICKERED TRAFFIC DIRECTOR at the Port Angelina ferry motioned me into the far right lane, behind a red Ford truck and beside a white minivan, both looking spanking new. Enough to give my battered little Civic an inferiority complex. I dutifully turned off my engine like the sign said and headed for the uppermost deck.

There'd been the usual hefty winter breezes on the island that day, but three decks up, the wind lashed at my face like the stingers of a jellyfish and sent my red windbreaker billowing behind me like Supergirl's cape.

I didn't feel like Supergirl. One case dropped, the other going nowhere. The microfilm search had netted nothing I didn't already know. Most of Bercain's appearances in the news were related to his run for mayor and the speculation about the governorship. Political enemies as assassins? They could be nasty but a bit high-profile to use murder as a tactic.

As the mainland loomed closer, my thoughts reluctantly shifted to my personal life—or the lack thereof.

As soon as I was in Gray's arms, though, all my recent doubts flew. He hung on as though he'd never let me go.

When his car wasn't in evidence at the house, I'd let myself in with my key. Ordinarily, I'd have headed straight for the bedroom and slipped into something *way* more

comfortable. I kept anything in the way of lingerie (as op-
posed to underwear) at Gray's, along with most of my
dressy clothes—such as they were. I had no use for either in
my island life, beyond the occasional *de rigueur* social event
to mingle with the moneyed for their future business. We
didn't go out much in Emerald either, being focused mostly
on being together.

But an instinct told me to soft-pedal the sexy tonight
until his initiation. And his first embrace reassured me that
whatever we were dealing with, it was not a shortage of love.

He, however, suggested we go out rather than up. "I'm
too pooped to cook," he said, "and I'm starving. Let's go
out. Something fancy. My treat."

That wasn't like him either; he liked to dress up even
less than I did. But I didn't object and went up to make the
lesser of my favored changes.

He stayed below, further cranking up my anxiety level. In
fact, when I thought about it, he was dressed quite formally
already. Instead of his usual cuff-frayed, elbow-patched tweed
sport coat, he was wearing the caramel-colored suede jacket
my parents had given him the Christmas before last and dark
brown pants I didn't recognize. My parents were wild about
Gray and fully in league with him to persuade me to trade my
jeans for an apron and a nursing bra. But they'd rather see
him behind a nice safe desk as well and kept giving us both
clothes we would have to elevate our lifestyle to make use of.
Not too subtle.

But I went along with it this time and put on the brown
velvet cocktail dress they'd presented me with at the same
time. Just two little moles in a hole we'd be. He didn't have
to wear heels with his, though, and I stood swaying on the
black patent-leather things, hoping I wouldn't disgrace myself completely by falling flat on my newly mascaraed face.

The restaurant was new to me: the Lobster Pot, on a bluff
some ten miles north of town, overlooking Possession Sound.

I could see the lights of Prince Island across the channel—a reverse and oddly disorienting vision.

We even had reservations, the maître d' nodding sagely to Gray's name and leading us to a window table. I wondered if that cost extra. I looked around, discreetly, as we walked. No mildewed nets and mounted salmon bodies here; the dark wood glowed in the candlelight at each table, and the chair the man pulled out for me was kid-glove leather to the touch.

When he bowed off, assuring us our waiter would be with us *toute suite*, I wondered aloud to Gray whether the man was a refugee from a French restaurant or if all people in the maître d' post at expensive restaurants were required to speak French. That netted me a familiar crooked grin and an unfamiliar kiss on the back of my hand.

"Higher," I said to that, but he just smiled.

The place was nearly full, but the tables were set just far enough apart that polite conversation probably could not be heard. I guessed that qualified as "intimate" in restaurant lingo. I'd have to watch my volume.

When the waiter came bearing menus that looked more like invitations to an exclusive soiree, Gray shortstopped my perusal (I love menus!) of the limited selections by saying, "Shall I order for us?"

Another first. I guess he took my startled silence for assent, because he said to the waiter, "Two lobsters *grandes*, two Caesar salads."

"It's their specialty," he explained when the waiter took my menu and left.

"Aha," I said. Had he been here before? Maybe I should think again before dismissing the possibility of another woman.

The food was a good diversion. The salads came first, which always annoys me. An excellent meal is one in which all the choices play off each other just right. That can hardly happen when you have to eat only one thing at a time. I chomped the romaine slowly, popped the croutons into my mouth one at a time, so there'd be some left for the lobster.

The lobsters, when they arrived, were definitely *grandes*. The plates were more like turkey platters. They didn't give us the usual bibs, so I fitted my linen napkin discreetly into the jewel neck of my dress and took hold of a claw in one hand and a silver cracker in the other.

I'd eaten both claws (and yummy ones they were!) before I glanced at Gray to discover he'd apparently been doing more grinning than eating. Gray always claims he likes to watch me eat. This goes directly against my parents' warnings throughout my childhood that if I didn't learn better table manners, no man would ever want me. I leaned to kiss him with my lobster-juiced mouth for proving them wrong.

The waiter had just left after lighting, then blowing out, the dessert flambé-whatever-it-was—one that apparently had been ordered when the original reservation was made—when it suddenly struck me. "You're going to propose!" I said to Gray. "That's what all this fancy stuff is about: You're going to propose again."

The smile faded from his face, leaving no expression there at all. I felt my own smile fade and my throat constrict, cutting off air. "Ohmigod," I said. "You're not. You're going to dump me. You've just been letting me down easy."

I jumped to my feet before he was forced to confirm my fears, tried to struggle into, then abandoned, the high heels I had slipped off once seated, and headed for the door, running from the voice he had finally regained.

Outside, only dim lights lit the restaurant entrance, and there were none at all in the parking lot. I began to run. Stupid! How could I have been so stupid!

Gray caught me halfway across the asphalt. I tried to

wrench from his hold on my arm, but he was stronger. "Molly! Stop! For heaven's sake, why would you ever think I'd dump you?"

I was more out of breath than the short run would account for. "Something's been wrong," I gasped. "For weeks now. Months. You obviously don't want me anymore."

Gray pulled me, somewhat roughly, into his tight embrace. I could feel every bone in his body, it seemed. It was as though he was the structure, I was the flesh. This was the same body that had pulled me back from the brink of extinction, and I'd relied on it more than I knew. The very thought of losing him was akin to the fear of amputation.

"Go wait in the car," he said. "I've got to go back and pay and get your shoes." He gave me a little nudge. "Go on, you're getting soaked."

That was the first I'd noticed how hard it was raining.

I did as I was told but dreaded his return. What was the point of reasoning out whatever was happening? He'd changed, and the result was distance. That was fact; everything else was just rationalization.

We didn't speak, really, until we reached his place. Then he was mostly anxious to get us both warm and dry. He ran the shower, took me in with him. But it wasn't foreplay, as it usually was. He scrubbed me as one might scrub a pet, then ordered me to put on his terry-cloth shaving robe, which on me was full-length. I'd used it often there, but it didn't usually stay on as long as I suspected it would this night.

He rubbed himself dry—every inch of himself, with uncharacteristic diligence—and put on some plaid flannel pajamas I'd never seen, before he came to the bed and faced me. "I know," he said, "things have seemed . . . a little off lately. But it has nothing to do with loving you. Or wanting you," he added, almost grudgingly.

The bed lamp was behind him, so his face was mostly in

shadow. I strained to see each flicker of expression that passed across it. There seemed to be a struggle among several emotions, but none I could quite pin down.

"Let me just tell you this," he said finally, his voice sounding strained. "You never have to worry—"

And his buzzer went off.

We both looked toward the foot of the bed, where his pager lay in the pocket of his pants.

"Damn!" he said, and grabbed it out, looked at it, and picked up the phone.

His conversation at my end was brief. "Yeah. Uh-huh. Who's there? Where's Galt? M.E. get there yet? Okay, I'm on my way." And he slammed the receiver into its cradle.

"I have to go," he said, already beginning to dress. "But I hope to get back before morning. When do you have to leave?"

Was I leaving? On Sunday? "Uh, early, I guess," I said.

"Stay here. Get some sleep. I'll be back as soon as I can."

I got no sleep, that's for sure. And the longer I lay there, smelling his spicy, warm smell, rerunning the intimacies we'd shared in this room, this bed, the crazier I was getting. Finally, as the sky outside the big dormer window was beginning to lighten, I was so wound up, I couldn't lie still another minute. I threw off the covers and got back into my jeans and sweatshirt and running shoes, grabbed my red windbreaker, and ran through the drizzle to my car, parked on the far side of the driveway. If I could just get away before he got back, I thought, it would be as though I'd stopped time. He and his secrets and his explanations would be frozen until I could deal with them. Whenever that might be.

I would go back to work. I would be on the active, not the reactive, side of my life, and that I could handle. I had to.

CHAPTER
9

I FOUND MAIA on the south side of the longhouse, raking leaves and moss from a wet patch of ground about six by seven feet, surrounded by tall Douglas firs. I could see another cleared patch, a little larger, some fifty feet behind it and to the north.

Maia had her back to me and seemed to be muttering to herself. All at once she raised the heavy rake and hacked at a stubborn piece of root with it as if it were a hoe.

I tried to ease up to her noisily, scuffing my feet in the leaves from a denuded alder, but I still startled her when I spoke. She whirled around, the rake raised, then looked embarrassed if not friendly when she recognized me.

She turned back to her raking—not difficult body language to decipher. I perched on a fallen log nearby to wait her out.

It must have been at least five minutes before she said, without turning, "Is this some game of chicken, to see who'll speak first?"

"I don't want to interrupt you," I said casually.

"Yes, you do," she snapped. "That's just what you want."

I didn't answer, and in a moment she turned to face me and said, "I'm sorry. I'm not usually this rude. In fact, I used to be quite a nice person." She slammed the rake against the ground and tried to clean between its stiff teeth with her muddy boot. "Before I lost every blasted thing I owned. Twelve years of hard work down the drain."

"Your home?" I said.

"*And* my business. *And* my marriage. Now what do I have?" Her gesture took in the bare ground, the rough long-house, and the drooping tents behind it. "Walden for losers."

I smiled, and in a moment she did too. "Well, it is. Anybody claiming this has high moral purpose is selling you a crock. It's the rich eating the poor, and all we've really got"—she gestured at the raked spaces—"is a couple of feet for lettuce and spinach. Which may or may not come up, considering the time it takes the sun to pass over it." She kicked one muddy boot against the other and sat down on a stump.

I could see she needed to unload, so I let her go at her own pace.

"You know? You do everything right, just the way the American Dream is supposed to go? You work at your little job until you have enough to build a little house. Then you go into business for yourself. Nothing big, nothing that's going to make you rich, just a little cottage industry. But it's enough for you. And you can hire a few others, provide enough income for them to be working toward *their* dreams. Then—" She made a slicing gesture across her throat.

I waited a few moments before I said, "Then?"

"Then your husband gets an early case of midlife crisis, and you're left with a house you can't finish, a business without its business partner, and a wide-open window for sharks."

"I take it Edmond Bercain was one of the sharks?"

"Big time," she said. "Bi-i-ig time. The man promised me—*promised* me, in what he assured me was a verbal contract just as binding as any written (and dumb me, I believed him)—that if I turned over fifty-one percent of the business to him"—she enumerated on the fingers of her left hand—"he would finance expansion and a catalog, would keep every one of my workers on, and keep the business located here in Grace."

"But he didn't," I said.

"Not for a minute. Before the ink was even dry on the deed of ownership, he was sending out work to Haitians, who had no choice but to work for less. *And* tax-free. Never *mind* quality. Had a fancy catalog designed, which meant raising prices to cover it, so he could sell to the idle rich who wanted to pat themselves on the back for supporting the arts and crafts. Then he closed down the Grace shop completely."

She was staring straight ahead, seeing something in her mind's eye. "The shop, the homemade goods, just weren't 'economically feasible,' he said. Not economically *fee*-sible. Like I would say, 'Oh, well then, never mind.' "

She glowered at her nails awhile, maybe the dirt under them, before I asked, "What kind of business was it?" Adding, "I've only been on the island a little over a year," to explain why I otherwise would have known.

"Patchwork," she said. "Everything patchwork. I started with quilts and pillows, selling through various retail outlets. Then I kept adding—skirts, toys, accessories. They were selling as fast as I could make them, and the stores wanted more. So I brought other women into it. And that worked great. I had a really nice group of women working with me. Out of their own homes mostly, especially new mothers who wanted to be home with their babies."

Maia broke off suddenly and leaned over with her elbows on her knees, her eyes hidden. I suspected tears. Loss or infertility? I waited for her to compose herself.

"*Then,*" she said finally, her chin jutting forward, "my business-genius husband thought we could be making more by opening our own shop." She paused. "And that was okay with me. I kind of liked the public contact. Even the tourists," she said with some surprise.

It had become clear to me by then that islanders tolerated tourists only for their dollars and heaved a sigh of relief when the season ended.

"It was nice to be offering what you made yourself," Maia went on. "Or your friends. The tourists kept telling us we could get twice our prices for our work in L.A. Or in Phoenix we could get rich on our tea cozies alone. But we were making enough; we were content with that.

"Until one fine day Eric decided that he needed more *space* in his life, more *challenge*, and decided *Alaska* was the only place he could get it. *Alaska!*"

She shook her head and lapsed into a ruminative silence. I waited.

"Eric always handled the business end: books, advertising, all that. I guess I appreciated that more once he was gone. When I realized I just wasn't going to make it on my own, I took out a second mortgage. Though I was barely making payments on the first. We built our own house from a log package, just the way we wanted it. Our dream home." Her tone was bitter. "I thought we'd have twenty years, easy, to pay it off. Think again."

She was staring into the woods, speaking in a distracted monotone. "A year later the business was in crisis again. Enter Edmond Bercain." She practically spit the name.

She turned toward me then. "I think the man must have an inside track at the bank. Had. Just when my balloon payment was coming due, up he popped. He'd do a catalog, he said. At his own expense, no risk to me. Yeah. Then it was, 'The bank wants me to co-sign on the shop to get the loan for the catalog.' Before I knew it the shop belonged to him, and I could get it back only by buying him out. Cash. After that, it was sheer dominoes." Her hand imitated a line of dominoes falling.

"What a sap!" She hit her chest with her fist, shaking her head in incredulity. "What a sap!"

I tried changing the subject. "Have the police been here?"

"Oh, yeah," she said. "Just after you left yesterday."

"Did they seem to see you as a suspect?"

"Who knows? They were polite. They asked a lot of questions. Then they asked them again."

"Just to you?"

"No, I think they questioned everyone here. But all separately. To see if our stories matched, I imagine."

"And did they?"

"I don't know. We didn't compare notes. I didn't anyway. I don't have all that much contact with people here. I do my 'chores' and stay in my tent. I should leave. I just don't know where or how to go." She made a harsh sound deep in her throat. "Maybe the police will make that decision for me." The second was harsher. "Wouldn't that be just perfect? He'd have gotten me good, even from the grave."

I was heading for the door of the longhouse to see who else was around, when Denny hailed me from the tent area. "Here you are again," he called. "Still on Bercain's payroll?"

I had to wonder whether his intent was to warn who-ever was inside the longhouse that I was coming and to make themselves scarce. I waited until he reached me before replying.

"*Mrs.* Bercain's," I said.

"Ah, the fascinating Ms. Kendall. I guess she's a rich widow now. Maybe I should pay her a call."

"Branching out into the gigolo business, are you?" I did not try to disguise my dislike for this cocky fellow. He seemed ninety-nine percent salesman to me, and I didn't trust the other one percent either.

"Touché." His smile remained cheerful. "Been talking to Maia, have you?"

"She hasn't much good to say about the late Mr. Bercain."

"Have you found anyone who does?"

"I haven't talked to everyone."

"Maybe his cronies in the campaign. They're probably frying all their fish together."

The remark reminded me that I hadn't had any breakfast and it was approaching lunchtime. "Anyone else around who might have had any contact with him?"

"Not that I know of."

He had been working himself around until he was now between me and the steps to the longhouse. I hadn't the energy for games. I pulled a card out of the pocket of my shoulder bag. "If anyone knows anything that might be useful, have them give me a call."

Denny grinned, knowing he'd won this round. "You betcha," he said.

My whole body was crying out for sleep. Even more than food. I climbed into my car and headed for home.

There were lights on in Free's cottage as I drove in. They cast a warm glow into the dreary day. I could use some cheering, I thought. It had been days since I'd found Free at home when I was. We were used to checking in with each other daily, and I missed that.

Free, for Freedom, is one of the most together persons I've ever known. A refugee from Seattle's stellar crowd, Free had accelerated her way through college and a business master's and had been asked to join the primo PR agency in the city. Their first black. But before a year was out she'd found life in the fast lane a drag and crossed the sound to the island, purchased five acres with a hunter's cabin on it at the edge of the woods. Shepherd's Woods is some thirty miles of forest, some still-virgin, which cuts down the middle of the island, separating East from West. (A few other factors do as well.) It is still a satisfyingly less-civilized place to be.

I'd met Free (the latest in a long series of name changes,

to fit her changing lifestyles) because she'd opened a small bookstore in Grace, which seemed to consist mostly of her own collection of volumes on African-American history and women's issues. It was more of a lending library, really, and I soon became her best lendee. When she found out I was living in the woods (in a tent at the time), she invited me to camp behind her cabin. Soon after, I purchased a wildly muraled homemade camper van from a New Age lad, and it has sat mostly concealed behind her cabin-becoming-cottage ever since. We're both pretty independent, but it's good to know someone else is within shouting distance in case of trouble.

Coming in the back door, I thought I could hear voices in the bedroom and proceeded through the kitchen into the living room, where some stunning progress was in evidence since I'd last been there. On the far wall, the crude fireplace had been covered by a neat brick face and hearth. Above it, a loft of freshly oiled maple skirted the chimney, gracefully rounded in front with a railing made of some dark polished wood.

I started up the sturdy maple ladder to see the view from up there, when Free must have heard my steps and called "Molly?" from the bedroom.

"Neat loft!" I called back, completing my climb and gazing about the room and through the arch into the kitchen. What a long way the place had come in Free's two years of transforming the bare-bones cabin into a cottage marked everywhere with her exquisite style. The broken glass had been replaced by many-paned windows scavenged from Seattle, and the back wall had been knocked out to accommodate a window seat at its center, softened with green velveteen pillows that echoed both the greenery outside and that in the green-and-gold stained-glass lamp hanging at one end. All made by Free herself, of course. So far I hadn't found a single thing she couldn't do. Made me feel like a klutz; I hadn't even gotten around to painting over the garish rainbow-cum-stars on the side of my funky camper.

I descended the ladder and walked into the bedroom, saying, "How did you ever get so much done since I was in here last?"

I stopped when I saw that she was packing, in the matching brown leather luggage she'd acquired in her flusher days. "You're going on a trip?" I said. "Well, about time you took a break. Are we talking exotic lands here?"

"New Zealand," a voice said, and I turned to see a woman coming out of the bathroom. She was blond and even taller than Free, who was a good five-foot-ten, with as well-muscled arms and shoulders as Free had developed during her heavy work on the house and garden.

"This is Judy," Free said quietly.

"Oh, yes, I think I've seen you helping Free with some of the heavy framing of the porch." I stuck out my hand. "Molly Piper."

She grasped it, with what seemed an unnecessarily firm grip.

"*We,*" she said, "are going where the sun still shines. And we're not coming back until planting time." She moved close behind Free, encircling her waist with an arm and kissing the top of her head.

I stared, first at the arm, then at Free's face. Surely, I thought, I must be misinterpreting this gesture and the possessive tone of the woman's voice. Surely Free would have told me if she were inclined toward women. We told each other everything. Didn't we?

"Please excuse us a moment, Judy," Free said. "I'd like to talk to Molly alone for a minute."

Judy smiled easily and left the room in no great rush.

"What's going on, Free?" I said. "Am I imagining—"

"No, you're not," Free said simply.

I didn't know where to begin. "Why haven't you ever told me? I mean, sexual preference is pretty basic, wouldn't you say, to one's self? I thought we were friends, that we were honest with each other." The words piled out but weren't nearly enough to express my hurt at being shut out of this part of her life. "Don't you *trust* me?" That was the essence of it.

"I suppose I don't trust much of anybody where this is concerned," she said. "I did once and got fired for it."

I tried to absorb what she'd just said. She got dumped from the PR job in Seattle? She didn't quit? But how was that even relevant?

"I am not just 'anybody,' dammit! I'm your *friend*. How could you even imagine I would not be fine with that? God, Free, I would still love you if you slept with apes and alligators!"

Free smiled at that, but I was not in a smiling mood. "I can't believe that you'd be so—" Words failed me, and I turned and pounded out of the house, past a smiling Judy.

Inside the camper, I threw myself on my bed and let the tears fall where they might. What was happening to my life? The two people outside my parents who were dearest to my heart didn't trust me with the truth?

It was some time before I heard Free's voice outside my slatted window vent. "I'm sorry, Molly, really. I should have known better. It's just—"

She didn't finish the sentence, but I grudgingly had to admit that I knew what it was "just." Coming out the last time had hurt her; she'd be more careful the next time. And the more people who knew, the more people who knew.

"Will you keep things watered for me while I'm gone?"

My voice came out harsh. "You think I'd let your babies die?"

"No," she said softly, "no, I don't." Then, "I love you, Molly, please believe that."

"I love you too," I said, and the tears started again.

CHAPTER
10

THERE WERE TWO THINGS I was dreading as I unlocked my office door late that afternoon: another "clue" from my mysterious tipster (I was in no mood for games), and a blinking light on my answering machine, which probably meant Gray was calling. Angry that I'd left before he got back. Telling me he wanted to break up.

There were both. I looked from the white envelope to the multiblinking light that indicated numerous calls.

Stalling, I opened the envelope first. At least it wasn't going to berate me in person. LIGHTHOUSE FOR FALSE LOVE, read the gaudy red and orange and green and purple letters. Terrific, I thought, and plopped into my swivel chair without removing my windbreaker.

I closed my eyes, going over the words. LIGHT-HOUSE. There was only one I knew of on the island, the Second Mate's Lighthouse at Brandy Point, no longer working. I went there now and then on summer evenings to gather my thoughts, scrambling barefoot out on the slick rocks to sit among the boulders, letting the sea lick my feet in a kind of baptism, the pounding of the waves reminding me that we are just Shakespeare's creatures strutting for a moment on the stage, full of sound and fury signifying nothing.

FOR FALSE LOVE. I guessed that brought me back to

the blinking light. Except that there was no way I could believe that Gray would be "false" in the sense of unfaithful.
Or even untruthful. Except maybe, like Free, in things left
unsaid.

The evening before had been running nonstop at the
back of my mind all day. Essentially, he had treated me like
a child. Grinning at my eating habits, taking charge when
I'd run out, taking me home and washing me like a parent.
Ordering me to stay put. All with no hint of awareness that
I was a grown woman and his lover for the past five years.

I had always blamed such caretaking behavior on my
size and went out of my way to assert myself as an adult.
Had I encouraged it somehow in Gray? I'd surely been a
wreck when he met me, in shock when he first came to the
hospital after my rape, then pretty much dysfunctional
later, when he took me in. It had been clear that sex was the
furthest thing from his mind; it was I who'd started it, so
sure was I that that life force would bring us both back to
life. Now what? No life force? No love? No nothing?

I punched the PLAY button on the machine, listened as
Gray's voice—first frantic, then carefully reasoning, finally
edged with irritation over the course of his messages—tried
to assure me of his continuing love and the need for commu-
nication. "Call me." "Call me." "Call me." *Now* he wanted
to talk. Well, I had a job to do.

When the tape had run its course, I punched both but-
tons simultaneously to erase and headed back out into the
drizzling rain.

At the lighthouse, still at some distance from the
housing clusters that surround the base on the western side
of the island, there was no one on the long strip of beach
in either direction. I heaved a sigh of relief and got out of
my car.

My feet seemed to know the way over the boulders
without much coaching from my brain, and I reached the
huge, lightless gray stone structure in moments, edging my

way around it and letting myself down into the wedge between two rocks that was my customary spot.

Compared to the spray that was tossed over me in the waves' steady splashings against the rocks, the light rain dwindled to insignificance—as did, in a way, my little worldly problems. Again the ocean brought me back to a sense of man's insignificance compared to nature's timelessness. A good thing? A bad thing? Just a fact, I supposed, but comforting somehow. Maybe because it signified a limit to how much we humans could mess up the planet. Not to mention ourselves and each other. Or maybe the rhythms of the sea were only whispering, *This too shall pass, this too shall pass.*

Is that what my relationship with Gray was doing? Passing, as all human bonds eventually must? Was I doing him—both of us, even—a disservice by wanting to hang on to the way things were? He was twelve years older than I. He wanted a family; I wasn't ready. Maybe it was just as simple as that.

There was a tightness in my chest I now recognized as a kind of panic, and it had been there for some time. Had I known I would lose him if I persisted in my own timetable without giving his equal time in my stubborn, selfish mind?

The only-child syndrome, my psych professor had called it in Human Development class. You get used to getting your own way, and some never give that up. It seemed I had heard that from my parents as well, more than once. Especially my father, who tended to give in to my whims when my mother wasn't present. "Don't tell your mother," he'd say, "or she'll blame me forever for spoiling you."

Forever. How could you conceive of, let alone plan for, forever?

Absorbed in my thoughts, I only gradually became aware of another sound playing counterpoint to the waves. It was a dull sort of clap, from somewhere behind me.

I hauled myself out from between the boulders and moved to the lighthouse, flattening my body against its water-smoothed stones, my arms spread in a clumsy embrace, returning counterclockwise around it.

The padlock to the rough old oak door was still in place. But as I watched, the door cracked open in the wind, then slapped shut again as another gust caught it from another direction.

I studied the padlock, hooked through the door's rusty hasp. I jiggled it; it seemed secure. But when I pulled down hard, the pin came out of its socket and the lock was open.

I lifted out the padlock, and the ancient door swung inward with an irritable creak.

I'd never been inside; the lighthouse had been shut down for years, I'd been told. But in the sudden absence of wind, the interior felt almost warm by comparison. Still, with no windows for the sun to shine through, the place was dank and smelled of rotting wood. So it was with surprise that I saw what appeared to be a pile of bedding on a ledge just past the iron stairway.

I approached to see a thick green foam pad laid on the wooden ledge, with a double sleeping bag atop it and two blankets of different shades of blue on top of that. With two yellow-and-white-stripe encased pillows at the head. What, the Martha Stewart rustic collection?

I felt the flannel lining of the sleeping bag, as though it might still be warm, and recognized the manufacturer's label attached to its slick burgundy shell. It was one of the choicest brands, guaranteed comfy to some pretty frigid temperatures.

Beyond the makeshift bed stood a silver candlestick, slightly tarnished, with a blood-red candle in it, burned about halfway down. I lifted the bedding, one piece at a time. No signs of mildew. When I got to the pillows, out of the nearest case dropped a packet of condoms, Super Trojan, also about half-empty. It would seem, I concluded, that this was a high-class, responsible, and rather recent little love nest. But for whom?

I pondered the question as I drove back to my office. If the author of my tipster notes was Mrs. Bercain, as I had been assuming, and they were intended to focus my investigation on Mr. Bercain's wrongdoings, did that make the love nest his?

But for the life of me, I could not picture that fastidious fellow grappling with some sweet young thing (isn't that always the object?) in an old dank and heatless lighthouse.

Who, then? Or was my informant someone else altogether?

I picked up a corned beef on rye and a lemonade at The Blue Heron and took it back to my office to eat. The café was packed, and friends beckoned me to their table, but I shook my head and pointed to my watch from across the room. My brain was playing leapfrog with my emotions, and I didn't need scrutiny. (How did that old song go? *They'd have asked me about you . . .*) Best to focus on work. Is this how workaholics are born? I asked myself.

CHAPTER
11

THAT EVENING, after the early dark of January, I secured my car behind some roadside brush across from the Second Mate's Lighthouse and opened a newly library-borrowed copy of Joy Fielding's *See Jane Run*. Scooting down in the seat, I laid my pen-size flashlight on what there is of my chest and angled it just right toward the book.

Jane was touring her unremembered house, an hour later, when a pair of headlights appeared from the east, jouncing down the unimproved road. (That night could have been worse: When you didn't jounce on that road, you wallowed.)

I quickly dumped the flashlight into my lap and clicked it off, peering through the dark to identify the vehicle. The headlights were high for a car and the motor was rough, probably a truck.

As it passed, I saw that it was indeed a truck, dark-colored and much-battered. It continued some fifty feet and pulled off on the other side of the road, ill-concealed behind a stand of lodgepole pines, their trunks pale in the light of a crescent moon as it slid between clouds.

I could barely see the shadowy figure that emerged from the driver's side of the cab, but as soon as it began to move, I recognized the jaunty gait: Denny Lockett.

I wasn't sure just why that surprised me. Surely he had

all the makings of a tryster—prone to breaking rules and dramatic gestures, with an ego that made him a soft touch for sexual flattery. Maybe it was only that I figured Denny must be supplied with plenty of females where he was. How far afield would he have to look? And why meet secretly? A married woman? Someone who couldn't afford to be seen with the town's bad boy?

The first woman who crossed my mind made me laugh out loud. Her Mayorship Ms. Stephenson-Roth. She certainly fit the category of mandatory secrecy. And she was attractive enough to be palatable, even at forty-something. Her position would make her a significant notch on the bedpost, even if it was a sleeping bag. But for the life of me, I couldn't picture it. Ms. Mayor in a bare and drafty lighthouse? Recklessly, I laughed again.

Meanwhile, Denny had made quick work of negotiating the rocks and was already at the lighthouse, where he was clearly silhouetted when the moon made it through the clouds again. It reinforced my hypothesis that it was the woman who more likely needed to keep the affair under wraps.

Who else? Over the next hour my guesses ran from Chief Belgium's wife, a surprisingly young and attractive bottle blonde; to Karen Pasco, the only woman so far on the island's police force; to any number of bored wives of military personnel at the Orson Naval Base some ten miles down the road on the island's west side.

But why would my informant clue me in to this little affair? If it was Kendall Bercain, why would she care? Only if she was the other affairee, I supposed. But why, then, would she want to expose her own affair?

Denny was, in fact, my second choice for informant, but the same applied to him.

Denny was still waiting, and I was still waiting by the hour's end—at 8:55 by the lit face of my digital watch—when I saw him stop his steady pacing and kick a boulder—

twice—then return over the rocks at a perilous pace to the shore. Moments later the truck's motor revved and the tires burned rubber, making a U-turn that raked my hiding place with headlights as it headed back from whence it came. Mr. Lockett, it seemed, was not a happy tryster.

I waited a discreet interval, then followed suit. Without the revving: My civil little Civic does not tolerate abuse or would have given up on me long ago.

I headed for home, making a note to get a Walkman for my next stakeout. While I had Jane's amnesiac wanderings to distract me, I could keep my mind off my own problems. Somewhat, at least. But sitting and staring for an hour, then driving and staring, gave the brain full permission to compulse. And compulse it did, replacing my professional questions of who and why with my own. Not a good trade. I resolved to narrow my focus to the case for the duration.

CHAPTER
12

AFTER A NIGHT OF FITFUL SLEEP, at best, I was in no mood for coy clues, and welcomed the white envelope lying on the floor of my office by slamming the door the rest of the way open, setting the metal file cabinet behind it reverberating. I snatched up the envelope, contemplating for a moment just ripping it up. I had neither time nor patience for this little game someone was playing. What did they want of me? "If it's you, Kendall baby," I barked out loud, "you can find yourself another detective!"

I threw the thing on my desk without opening it and went to make tea. My third cup of chamomile that morning. So far its famed soothing properties weren't working.

I rocked back and forth in my squeaky swivel chair, staring at the innocuous white envelope before I grabbed it and slit its throat.

WHITEHOUSE, it read, on a triangular piece torn from what looked like a newspaper headline.

"So what are you telling me, buddy?" I shouted. "The President did it?"

The next thing I knew, T-om was standing in the open doorway. "You okay?" he asked.

I stared at him, marveling again that he could go through an entire winter wearing only his habitual yellow loincloth. I'd been relieved that none of those coming up the stairs to his meditation classes seemed to feel similarly obliged. Although maybe beneath their coats, each and every one . . . I shivered at the thought.

"Sure," I grumbled in answer to T-om's question. "Just dandy."

He looked as though he might settle in for an advice-giving session, so I forced a smile. "Really," I said, and held it until he reluctantly withdrew.

I tried to focus on work, away from the machine no longer blinking, but with little success. Everything in my head seemed to be at war, and the clamor was deafening.

I knew only one way to clear it and hit the street running.

Under a mottled sky I ran the familiar streets, passing the People's Drugstore on Nutmeg, the WonderWoman plus-size clothing store as I cut through to Parsley.

As I paused at the top of the switchback stairway, the beach looked strangely barren. The sand uncovered by the receding tide was littered with empty shells and chunks of driftwood in a pattern that bore no resemblance to anything I remembered seeing there before. True after each high tide, I told myself, but it didn't seem to explain it. Even my ocean was deserting me.

As I descended the last slippery stairs, I heard a screech, like that of a seagull—close—then broke out onto the sand to see a child up the beach at the water's edge, rushing after the foam of a receding wave.

It screeched again, its hands slapping the water, then turned to run ahead of the next wave up the sand.

Emily. For a bad moment I thought she might be there alone, from what I'd heard of her mother. Then I saw Mikah, sitting on his usual rock before The Faces, but facing his sister's dance. I glanced at my watch: well past time for school.

Mikah saw me, put up a hand in salute. I did the same.

"No school?" I said when I was within hearing distance.

He gestured toward Emily. "Mom didn't come home last night," he said dully, as though he'd said it often.

I didn't respond, just perched on my nearby rock and absently stared at The Faces. What a crock, I thought, seeing some momentous message in the chance lodgings of salt in the crevices of some old carvings on a seawall. Irrationally, it made me mad.

"You wanna run?" I said to Mikah, and took off for the water's edge.

He must have been dealing with some anger himself, because he came pounding right behind me, scooped up Emily, and had nearly caught up by the time I got to the PRIVATE NO TRESPASSING sign.

I won't repeat what I said to it, but it's often called the *F* word and ends with *you*!

I glanced at Mikah. It was the first time I'd seen his smile, much less the grin he was wearing.

"Pirate!" Emily said, pointing at the sign.

I looked at Mikah, amazed. "She's talking!" I said.

"I teach her some words," he answered carefully. "Private," he corrected her.

Emily pointed to the house on the cliff. "Pirate!" she said again. And he corrected her again.

I turned, the urge to run gone, and began trudging back toward the stairs.

"Would you want to come see my room?" Mikah asked suddenly from behind me.

I turned, hardly believing my ears. This remote, defensive boy was inviting me to his home?

"Okay," I said. "Sure."

CHAPTER
13

THE METAL SCREEN DOOR banged behind Mikah as he swung Emily from his back to the floor in a well-practiced move.

Emily landed running and went straight to the kitchen table, where she climbed up a wobbly chair and stood upright on her knees, apparently ready for the lunch she'd been demanding since we left the beach.

"Moo-moo-moo-moo" meant food, Mikah had informed me as we cut up Pansy Street to Sand Run Road, then down an alley to a lineup of soiled sky-blue apartments. I'd never noticed them before, though they stood just behind my favorite restaurant, The Galleon.

Mikah opened the refrigerator, and a waft of sour air swept out. He didn't have to keep it open long, though, its meager contents making decisions none too difficult. Mikah backed up with a half loaf of white bread in one hand, a plastic package of lunch meat in the other, a carton of milk tucked under his left elbow.

He deposited them on the table. But it took one whiff of the milk to convince him that it was better poured into the sink, where it gave off virulent fumes even after he'd run a blast of water to wash it down.

I didn't even want to see the lunch meat and was happy to decline when he offered to make me a sandwich as well.

I settled in the chair across from Emily's at the grimy white table and watched as she focused intently on her brother's making of the sandwiches.

The child was a study in contrasts. Her mop of unbrushed golden curls dangled over milk-chocolate eyes, but her perfect rosebud mouth didn't seem to fit above a strong jaw and wide shoulders too big for her toddler body. I'd have said her upper features must resemble her mother and the lower the father of them both. Except that Mikah had said the two had different fathers.

"Turd!" she began chanting now. "Turd!" And Mikah pulled open the refrigerator door again and withdrew a capless plastic jar of mustard, poking at it with a knife to break through its stiff black crust to let a dribble of yellow seep onto the bread.

"Tuc!" Emily ordered as he set her sandwich before her on a half-square rip of paper towel from the roll on the table.

Mikah cut her sandwich in half.

Cut, I thought, wondering whether there was such a thing as dyslexia of the spoken word, where all the sounds come out backward.

Mikah sat in the third of the three chairs at the table and started telling me about the items in his bedroom he had invited me to see.

"My father's an archaeologist, see," he said. "All his life he's been studying the history of our people, the Makah tribe. They lived in this region long before the white man came." His face darkened, as though the very mention of "the white man" was enough to plunge him into depression. Emily watched his face too, as her teeth made short work of her sandwich.

"This dig," he went on, "that my father was part of was in Makah territory below Neah Bay. A village called Ozette." He pointed west, in the general direction of the Olympic

Peninsula. "There had been a mud slide there, we think," he continued eagerly. "So it preserved stuff like wall planks and roof supports and even baskets and rope that usually would have rotted by now. It was a very important dig, and of course our people were part of it. The Makah Tribal Council watched over the whole thing. They'll be building a special museum to display all the things they found, so everyone can learn the Makah ways and admire their art."

As though he could wait no longer, Mikah stood and, with the last bite of his sandwich in his mouth, said, "Come on, I'll show you. It's all in my room."

That seemed to be Emily's cue to follow her brother, and she clambered from her chair, clutching the last half of her sandwich, which I noticed was dripping mustard onto the green shag of the carpeting in the next rooms. From the looks of the trail, it was apparently not the first time.

We passed through a small room that was probably meant to be a dining room, but was vacant except for a glassed curio cabinet that held a collection of Barbie dolls dressed for the beach, the ball, the kitchen, the tennis game, the skiing trip. . . .

The front door was beyond that, in a little entrance hallway, from which a staircase led to the second floor, both hall and stairs covered with the same nearly nubless lime-green shag.

At the foot of the stairs was a small dusty table, on which lay an assortment of mail, unopened. The sight of mail makes a detective's fingers itch, and I paused, looking at what I could see of it without touching anything. Mostly bills, it looked like, some with postmarks months old.

"Molly?"

Both kids had reached the second floor, and I sprinted up to join them.

Mikah was standing in the doorway of the room to the left of the landing, and he stood aside for me to enter.

It was much like any teenager's room—discarded clothing on the floor, stacks of books by the bed, a desk piled with a jumble of papers. But in this teen's room the walls were filled not with posters of rock stars and supermodels but with small framed black-and-white photographs on the near three walls. And on the long wall over the bed, various wooden objects were propped on heavy nails driven into the wall on which they leaned.

He pointed to the pieces on the wall. "I made them," he said proudly. "From the photographs my father took of each piece he discovered. Before," he added darkly, "the university could take them. They take everything our people have."

Mikah gave his head a couple of shakes, as though to clear it of disturbing thoughts, and directed his attention back to the objects. "Now these are part of our history too, made by a Makah, his son, to show the ways of our ancestors." His arm described an arc encompassing the room, and his wide face shone.

I drew closer to study the pieces, leaning as far as I could over the bed. The wood was nearly white.

"I made them out of driftwood," Mikah explained, "so they would look old, like the real ones. Western red cedar. Everything the Makah made—all the houses, the tools, the canoes—everything was made of Western red cedar. Our natural wealth, they called it. Even the clothes were made of cedar bark."

He pointed to a rough shaft mounted diagonally on the long wall above the bed. "That's a harpoon," he said. "Ten feet long. The Makah men were great whale hunters. And brave! They used to steer their canoes right up to the side of the whale and spear him." Mikah demonstrated, pointing to his shoulder blade. "You had to get him right behind the flipper. Very dangerous! Then they had to paddle backward fast, or the whale's tail when he dived would cut the canoe in two and they would all be drowned."

Mikah's face was so animated, compared to his usual guarded, sullen look. I couldn't take my eyes off him.

"They weren't like hunters now, who just kill for fun. Or money. They used every bit of the whale. The men and whale were equal, both strong. The women would pray to the whale to come to their hunters. People lived equal with the animals then. And the land."

He reached to a narrow shelf over the head of the bed and picked up two pieces of what looked like bone, each half a foot long, cut in a zigzag pattern. "Barbs for the harpoon," he said. "My father made a list of everything he found."

I noticed another shaft toward the foot of the bed. Not as long, and thicker, it ended in a bulbous profile, with an eye and snub-nosed mouth—maybe a snake's head? I pointed toward it.

"Ka-tum," Emily said. She had pulled herself onto the bed and was closely following the movements of her brother and myself.

"Seal," Mikah translated. "*Katum* is the Makah word for seal. I'm teaching my sister Makah, so when she decides to talk she can use that language if she wants."

He moved toward his desk as I stood on tiptoe, noticing that the features of the seal in profile looked like a morose human face when viewed from above.

Mikah lifted a sheaf of papers from the desk. Down the left side were English words, followed by markings that looked like hieroglyphics. "This is how you say things in Makah. It doesn't translate very well, so you have to just go by the sound. My father sends them to me, in his letters."

He moved to the photographs, each framed behind smudged glass, as though many hands had touched it—or one hand many times. "My father took these," he said. "He gave them to me just before they took him away to prison. So I would know my history and my Makah family.

"The interior of a communal lodge," he said, pointing

to one that looked not unlike the Squatters' longhouse, except for the smoke holes in the ceiling. "Everyone used to live together like this. And each one had a job. So they were never broke or alone."

I was drawn to a photo near the door that showed a man sitting on a woven mat, painting a mustache on the upper lip of a large and quite handsome mask. The man frowned as he worked, his own mustache following a downward curve similar to that of the mask, his brows knit in concentration.

"That's my uncle Attlu," he said. "My father's brother. He's the best maker of ceremonial dance masks of our people. You see that medal he wears? It was given to him by the Canadian government.

"This," Mikah said, pointing to another, "is me, a few years ago. I was ten maybe." His finger touched the last boy in a line of five, all holding what looked to be wooden spears. The face Mikah indicated was out of focus, staring with a bit of a scowl. "We were dancing," he said. "Indian dances, on Makah Day.

"And here," Mikah announced in a climactic tone, drawing me by the elbow to the wall over his desk. "This is my father. On the right here." He pointed to a dark-haired young man, maybe thirty, wearing a suit jacket and jeans. "When he was chairman of the Tribal Council. They had to approve everything the university people did on that dig."

Mikah's thumb caressed the bottom of the frame. "I don't know what I'd do without my father's letters," he said, so quietly I almost didn't hear.

"How long has he been in prison?"

Mikah's face darkened further. "All my life. Seems like."

"When will he be coming home?"

Mikah shook his head and didn't answer for a while. Then his tone was low, bitter. "Who knows? When an Indian goes after a white man, they just lock you up forever."

"Whom did he 'go after'?"

"One of those university guys, who was going to take our treasures."

"Did he kill him?"

Mikah shook his head impatiently. "My father just gave him what was coming to him."

CHAPTER
14

WHEN I GOT BACK to the office, I called Dale Eppes at the Take-A-Hike store in Port Angelina.

"Long time, Moll," he said when I identified myself. "When they move from a tent to an RV, they forget you."

I laughed dutifully. "I need some info. It's a long shot, but you're the only camping-supplies outfit on the East Island, so I thought maybe you'd know."

"Not too flattering, but shoot."

"Did you sell a double sleeping bag anytime within . . . oh, the last year, probably?" I gave him the manufacturer and a description.

"Well, it's more than you deserve, but in fact I did. I remember because it was the only double I had. Don't get too much call for them."

There is such a rush when you connect with just the information you need. "My breath is bated," I said.

"I could pun that," Dale said cheerfully, "but you don't sound in the mood. I don't think I can give you a name, but I remember the lady. Walked in wearing designer sweats, but the sweat was real. Tall, looked like she could hold her own in a bar fight."

"Thirties? Black hair?"

"You got it. That the answer you wanted?"

"I don't know yet. Thanks, though, Dale, I owe you one."

I sat with the phone receiver in my hand, the connection broken. Why would Kendall Bercain send me off to her own trysting spot?

Watch those assumptions, my mentor's voice reminded me. He said it often because I forgot it often. He was right: I had no real reason to believe that Kendall was my informant. And even if she were, her buying such a sleeping bag didn't make her the one who used it. There were things stolen from her house.

But if she didn't, who?

I released the button on the receiver and got a dial tone. I knew my client's number by heart.

This time it was, "*La señora* no here." At least it was better than "no talk." I left my name and number. But why did I think she wouldn't use it?

When in doubt, stake out.

Every time I do a daylight surveillance, I am reminded that my car is not exactly nondescript. For stakeouts you want an old black Ford, or a middle-aged Chevy, innocuous blue. My aged Honda Civic hatchback, on the other hand, is probably unique in all Autoland. Brown on the bottom, oxidizing tan on top and every other fender, it looks like a Reese's Cup that has been in Mike Tyson's pocket too long. The little-old-lady I bought it from when I arrived on the island said her grandson had painted it that way; but from the twinkle in her eye, I suspected her of being a closet Reese's Cup addict.

So why don't I ever quite get around to repainting it some solid, dark, dowdy color? Who knows? I'm sure it has nothing to do with my similar love for chocolate and peanut butter in the same bite.

I parked the little bugger behind some trees well past

the driveway to the Bercain home and breached a very prickly hedge to reach the lawn on foot and come up on the far side of the house, just past the garage. At least it had stopped raining, I consoled myself, as I settled into a fresh pile of dead leaves to await whatever.

It wasn't long before I realized that I was smelling more than decomposing leaves beneath me. I identified the orange rinds and discarded steak fat by smell before I eased off the pile and poked at its contents with a stick. "Oh, great," I muttered; save the planet and all that, but couldn't she at least keep her compost in a bin?

I was spared further environmental slander by the approach of a vehicle. I stepped back nearer the garage as a forest-green Lexus whipped up the drive and braked just yards from me.

The driver didn't bother to shelter the car. There were brisk steps across the gravel, skirting the island planting of budded rhododendrons, and up the brick steps to the front door.

I chanced a peek. My client's long lean figure was clad in black jeans, a black turtleneck, and a red windbreaker not unlike mine. I didn't know whether the black was intended to be a gesture of mourning or just plain sexy, but my money was on the latter. Still in need of validation after a loveless marriage?

In a moment she had unlocked the door and passed inside. I debated following but decided that would make the stakeout pretty obvious unless I waited a decent interval. Which I was not wild about doing next to the ripe garbage pile. So I headed back to my car and its cell phone.

"Tell her it's Molly Piper," I said.

"*Señora*—" was as far as the housekeeper got before Kendall came on the line.

"Yes? What do you have for me?"

I decided to go on the offensive. No press, no confess. "My question relates more to what *you* have for *me*. If you have information I would appreciate your telling me directly rather than in cryptic notes."

There was a small pause. "You've been getting notes?"

"You've been sending notes?"

"Why would I do that?"

"Took the words right out of my mouth."

"So what do they say, these notes?" Kendall asked cautiously.

I could not believe I hadn't decided whether to tell her if she maintained ignorance of the notes. I hoped my snap decision was the right one. "The first said *Truth in Advertising*, the second *Twisted Times*, the third *Lighthouse for False Love*, and the last one *Whitehouse*."

There was a long pause. Then, "And you think these have to do with the murder of my husband?"

"I doubt they relate to either of the cases I just closed," I said.

"So how do you interpret them?"

"I asked you first."

Silence. Then, "I don't know anything about notes. But if you have questions I will try to answer them."

"Question one," I said. "Do you know a counter-culture hunk named Denny Lockett?"

"I've heard of him," she said carefully.

"That's not what I asked. *Know,* as in personally. Biblically."

"Why would you ask?" Ever-cool.

"Because apparently it's germane to the case."

"I don't see how."

"Yes or no, please."

"We became friends at one time," she said slowly.

"Lighthouse-rendezvous kind of friends?"

"How do you know that?" Her tone had lost its cool.

"Among other things, the purchase of a double sleeping bag."

"That is over." Her voice was tight.

"For you or him?"

"I don't see— For me. I have ended it."

"Before or after your husband was killed?"

"I resent that implication! I've told you, Denny had nothing to do with my husband's death. None of those Squatters did, I'm sure."

"And *I* told *you*, I have to be free to explore every possible line of investigation."

"Then 'explore'!" she snapped. "And tell me what you find." And she broke the connection.

I reviewed the conversation as I drove back to the office. Now, I supposed, the question was: Did I believe her? The patrician and the pauper—go figure. Except that Kendall Bercain didn't exactly fit the definition of patrician. Nor did the savvy Lockett make a very convincing pauper. Maybe what they had was a common enemy. Lovers? Conspirators? Killers?

But if Kendall wasn't my informant, who was? Denny wanted me to witness his humiliation at being stood up for his tryst at the lighthouse? I didn't think so. And I couldn't come up with a single reason Kendall would want to advertise an affair with a callow youth such as Denny Lockett.

But, then, she had married Edmond Bercain, hadn't she? How much knowledge of good men could she have?

I climbed the stairs, trying to divert my mind from the subject of good men. I began to replay the scene of our last evening together. He said, I said . . . Then I should have said . . .

"Don't go there," I warned myself aloud as I unlocked the door and seated myself at my desk without removing my windbreaker.

I pulled an 8½-by-11-inch pad out of my lower left drawer. I'd been so distracted by the notes and my own problems, I'd forgotten to follow my usual routine in pursuing a case. In the hope that an organized case produces an organized mind, I usually use one of those brown six-pocket accordion files and keep jotting down what I discover as I discover it, filing them in pockets labeled *People*, *Suspects* (moving one to the other as I went), *Locations*, *Possible Clues* (the tangibles), *Hunches* (the intangibles), and *Data*, all the bits and pieces gathered along the way that hadn't yet announced where they fit. I had neglected to buy a file for this case but labeled the sheets accordingly and began writing.

My *People* list was a broadening exercise. I'd been so focused on Kendall as suspected author of the notes that I'd looked less critically at others. As authors *or* killers.

I made a separate sheet for each of the Squatters—Denny, Maia, Sam, Iris, Frank, Leonard, Dorothy, her daughter. Had anyone told me the daughter's name? And what about the husbands? Carl—was he Iris's? And Maia's? Eric? (This is why you keep lists, so you don't forget anybody.) I'd have to be sure Eric was still in Alaska and Carl in Virginia when the murder went down. Who knew what-all grudges or guilt projections could have been festering in those two?

And then there were Bercain's business and political associates. If he'd played as fast and loose with others as he had with Maia, that might be a sizable body of suspects.

I rummaged in my bag for the list of those I'd jotted down during my hours at the microfilm goggles.

Alan Gartrell, loan manager at the Island Savings and Loan. Maia had mentioned a possible "inside track" at a bank. Gartrell? I'd spotted him in a group photo of Bercain's big-money political supporters. Others were Darrin McBroom, owner of The Market, Grace's food-and-more store; Oran Kamholz, head of Kamholz Construction, big landholder on the East Island; and Betty Brattleford Jarrett, widow of Richard P. Jarrett, former chairman of the Island Republicans.

The latter lady could also figure as one of the business-or-pleasure suspects Kendall had specifically requested that

I target. I had jotted down the names of women who'd appeared with Bercain in social-event pics in the *Grace Guardian* over the last year. Jarrett appeared in four such photos; Sandy Gartrell of Gartrell Realty, three; Suzette Ayerling on the Town Council, three. Goldie Franklin, older but rich, appeared in two; and Sylvia Beers, philanthropist, in one.

But it was the mayor herself, Marion Stephenson-Roth, who had been observed in the most such photo ops: no less than seven. Unable to run for a third term, the mayor seemed to have chosen Bercain as her worthy successor, and that put her at the head of that list and my necessary interviews.

I was not looking forward to it. As I said, Maid Marion was not one of my favorite pretentious people. Maybe if I hadn't spent so much time in a Big City with all its problems, I'd have been more impressed with her mayorship, but I had and I wasn't. At least not as much as she was.

Probably partly as a stall, I opted to make another visit first. Iris had mentioned working at a diner, and it was lunchtime. I headed for The Last Diner, a fifties sort of place with jukeboxes at the booths and soda-fountain stools at the counter, situated at a key location on Nutmeg, just before Daisy.

It was high noon, and the diner was packed, with business lunchers as well as the regulars who could be found there just about any time of day. I often wondered what they did for a living that they could just hang out at their leisure. I nodded to a few in the booths but took a counter seat myself. I had spotted Iris picking up an order at the window and was hoping for a few minutes of chat.

Before I could snag her attention, though, a deep voice from two stools down on my left said, "We meet again."

I leaned forward to see past the person between us and was confronted by the bearded face of Sam, who regarded me with an amused look, as though he'd been waiting for me to show up.

Before I could respond, he had asked the woman between us if he could switch with her and had settled onto the stool next to mine with as much cockiness as if he'd been invited.

"Solve your case yet?" he asked, and smiled at my frown.

"My case is now murder, and you're my chief suspect," I replied, for no reason other than my irritation at his manner. I was not long on tolerance that day.

"You found me out," he said cheerfully.

My head turned to follow Iris as she maneuvered her way around the end of the counter and through the haphazard arrangement of tables in the center to a window booth, where she set down her tray and began distributing its contents. The window afforded as clear a view of Nutmeg as I remembered, but none of Daisy.

"Iris didn't do it," Sam said.

I turned back with some surprise. "Is there any reason for me to suspect that she did?"

The big man shrugged. "Course not," he said, but the smile was gone.

"Did Iris know Bercain?"

Sam concentrated on the salt shaker his big hands were rolling between them like a joint. "We all did, one way or another. He came around with a fella from some bank a few times, looking to buy right before their foreclosures by other banks were finalized."

"Was the bank Island Savings and Loan?"

"Yeah, I think that was it."

"Was the loan officer named Alan Gartrell?"

"Maybe. I didn't pay much attention; I never owned any property in the first place."

"But one of the properties was Iris's?"

"Her and that worthless husband of hers."

Sam was avoiding eye contact. Could it be that he was sweet on the woman? I looked at her again. She had the stooped shoulders of a woman who'd grown too fast too young and tried to minimize her height. She was painfully thin, and her pale coloring and awkward movements made her seem fragile, if not downright sickly. Maybe, I thought, Sam had a tender, protective side to his nature that was not obvious at first meeting. Could those feelings have led to murder?

"What about her husband?" I asked. "Has he been back to the island at all? Have you met him?"

"Nah," he said darkly, "he'll never be back." Then Sam added, "Not if he knows what's good for him."

The mocking smile returned as one of the other waitresses, a worn, overweight blond woman, appeared before us, tapping her pencil against her pad. "You know what you want?" she said to me. Apparently Sam had either already ordered or was a low-spending regular to be ignored. A mug of creamed coffee was the only thing he had moved over with him.

"What's your soup?" I asked, not wanting to take the time to refresh my memory of their menu.

"Black bean. And our usual chowder."

"Okay. Cup of black bean and a grilled cheese."

"On?"

"On . . . wheat, whatever."

"We have rye," she said, as though giving me another chance to make the right choice.

"Rye's fine," I said, and she made a note as she turned to spike the order on the turntable for the kitchen staff.

"So," I said to my de facto lunch partner, "what's going on at the camp?"

He shrugged. "Same old same old."

"Which is?"

"Work, schemes, squabbles . . ."

"Schemes?"

"Figure of speech," he said quickly.

"Such as the WANTED posters and the break-in?"

Sam's mouth curved in the same mocking grin. "Would we do that? That would be illegal."

"Maybe the scheme escalated."

"To murder? None of them have the balls for that."

"Not even Denny?"

"Especially Denny," he said with disdain. "He's all talk."

I tried another tack.

"So who are the other in-house couples?"

He caught the implication of "other" and gave me a sharp look, but he answered the question. "Probably everybody, at one time or another. The pickings are pretty slim."

"Denny?"

"Denny and just about every woman there. Started in on the kid too, but Dorothy put a stop to that."

"The teenager? Is she Dorothy's daughter?"

"Yeah. Name's Amber. Just turned sixteen."

"So off-limits."

"Tell *her* that. She's shaken it at every guy within striking distance."

"But you all resisted?"

"Hey, you get a good look at her? As I said, the pickings are slim. She moves on, though. Short attention span."

Iris came back around the counter. This time she noticed me and gave a small frown.

I smiled. "I was just wondering if anybody from the camp was in town on New Year's Eve. Were you working then?"

Iris shot a look at Sam, then said, "Yeah. It was my usual night."

"How long's your shift?"

"Till ten usually. But we worked longer that night. Because of the parade and all."

"How long?"

"The police already asked that," she hedged.

"They don't share with me," I said. "And I'm working for Mrs. Bercain now."

Iris shifted her weight, as though to give the other foot a rest. "It was only supposed to be until midnight. But it took a long time for the buses to take everybody off, so we were packed for hours. And then some of 'em were drunk, so Stan decided to serve breakfast."

"And did you see anything? Or hear anything, around midnight?"

"The noise in here, I wouldn't've heard a bomb drop."

I turned to Sam. "How about you? How long were you here that night?"

"Just until—" Then he realized the trap but went on anyway. "Iris gave me some breakfast. About one or so. I'd been drinking pretty hard, at Frankie's. Then I waited till she was done and drove her home."

"About when was that?" I addressed Iris.

Sam and Iris exchanged a look.

"About . . ." Iris said slowly, "two? Or three?"

Sam nodded without commentary. Iris turned quickly and took two plates from the kitchen delivery counter and carried them off without another glance at us.

I said to Sam's lowered head, "You mentioned that Denny's been with just about everybody?"

He seemed disinclined to follow my lead. But after several moments of silence he said, "Denny's basically an asshole. He gets an itch, he scratches, doesn't matter who gets ripped."

"And was Iris one of those who got 'ripped'?"

"He got around to her eventually," Sam said, trying to keep the emotion out of his voice but not quite succeeding.

"Who else?"

"Well, Maia was first, of course."

"Of course?"

"The only one he considered his equal. At least *he* thought so."

"You didn't?"

"*She* didn't, more to the point. They got into it, yeah, but she saw through him pretty quick."

"In what way?"

The big man shrugged. "There's something . . . I don't know. Like what's-wrong-with-this-picture. Something just doesn't fit." He frowned into his empty coffee mug. "He's too quick, too ready with the answers. Like he's got some sort of agenda, beyond the camp and everything. I don't know."

He gave me a sideways glance, as though he expected me to pounce on that. But I decided I might get more if I just let him talk.

"I don't even know how long he's been on the island or where he came from. First I saw of him was last winter. Maia had just lost her shop, about six months after Eric left. And there he came, the white knight to the rescue. I think the rest of us are just along for the ride."

"Sounds like you see a lot of what goes on in Grace."

"I've been around a while. Most of the last eight years, I guess. It's a small town."

"And no one knows why he came?"

"Not that I ever heard. First I saw him was with Maia. Then he came up with the camp idea. It wasn't hard finding people who'd been screwed over by the system. The whole thing seemed to just spring up overnight. At least by island time."

The island prides itself on its slow pace compared to the rest of the country. Sometimes I think it's just wishful thinking. But, then, my profession is not exactly laid-back.

"That takes a lot of charisma," I said, "to get that many people moving so fast."

"Oh, he's got that, all right. That and an ego as big as my butt."

I smiled at the simile. "So were the WANTED posters his idea too?"

Sam grinned and pointed a thumb-and-forefinger gun at me and pulled the trigger. "Not twice in one day," he said. "That's what we've got the Fifth Amendment for."

I shifted my tack. "Did Denny ever bring Kendall Bercain out to the camp?"

Sam's heavy eyebrows arched, widening his light blue eyes. "You have been busy."

Then he placed both palms on the counter and pushed himself upright. "I think I hear my mother calling. She always told me not to talk to strangers."

CHAPTER
15

I SPENT THE REST OF THE WEEK going down my list of *People*, to see who should be moved to the *Suspects* list. I eliminated Kamholz—away on vacation at the time, as were Ayerling and Franklin. I kept Jarrett, McBroom, and Beers on the list, though none in my brief interviews rang my alarm bell as serious suspects. Two were currently out of town: Gartrell and Her Mayorship, so I put their sheets in my *Hold* box.

All in all, I tried to keep myself very busy and hold at bay all thoughts of the future. Gray had stopped calling; I considered it an impasse. I filled the void with food and exercise.

Early Saturday morning I pulled on jeans and running shoes and took off on my usual route through the woods. The circuitous, unmarked path was so familiar that I could put myself on automatic and still make the jumps over fallen trees and gullies without having to concentrate, which would have been impossible. It was only when I reached the burned remains of the cabin where I'd witnessed a ritual killing that I was caught up short. I didn't need to see that now.

I did a U-turn and ran back. But when I came in sight of

my camper again, I still had nervous energy to burn, so decided to keep on going. The Squatters' camp was only three or four miles to the north, and I'd forged a path of sorts there the previous spring, so thought I might as well go in the back way and see who might be home and in an informative mood.

I heard the voices just as I was about to break through the dense underbrush on the south side of the longhouse. They seemed to rise and fall like a fitful tide: *murmur-murmur-murmur-yell, yell-murmur, murmur-murmur-murmur-yell, murmur-yell-murmur-murmur . . .*

I squatted there just short of the clearing and found that when my labored breathing eased, I could make out the voices.

Denny's was saying, "I know for a fact Kendall told her to lay off the robbery investigation and us as suspects in the murder."

"I'm sure you do," a low voice said. I couldn't quite place it.

Maia's I recognized, yelling, "I don't care; I want all the stuff out of here. Send it to the people you said you would—just get it out of this camp. Molly Piper isn't the only one investigating both crimes, you know."

Denny: "Crimes, plural? You sure saw the whole Brigade operation as righteous at the time. You were, in fact, one of the originators of the idea, as I recall."

"That was before it turned to murder."

"*Turned to murder?* Is that what you think? You think *I* killed *Bercain*?"

The third voice said, "Let's face it: Any of us could have done it. But it's not going to help for us to wrangle like this." Dorothy's even tone I recognized this time.

"Exactly," Denny said. "We've got to hang together on this. There's nothing the cops would like better than to bust us for *something*. Anything. This camp is a thorn in their side. All the Establishment crowd in Grace."

"Knock off the sixties rhetoric," a voice I recognized as Frank's said. "I swear you talk like you've been frozen in time for the last three decades."

"We can learn a lot from them," Denny said hotly. "At least they *believed* in something and had the guts to *act* on it. Not just a bunch of malcontents whining because they got screwed by the system. I mean, get in line, you know?"

From a distance came the low hum of a motor—not loud enough to be a car and not from the direction of the camp's makeshift parking lot to the east.

It seemed to be coming from the north, along the path from the fairgrounds, so I edged counterclockwise around the clearing until I could see its line of approach, careful to remain hidden in the underbrush.

Breaking into the escalating hum from within, Denny's voice yelled suddenly, "Stop! What's that? Quiet!" and the voices inside stuttered to a halt as Denny came shooting through the front door.

Before the thing even came into view, there was the sound of an angry voice cursing up a storm, all but drowning out the drone of the motor.

Then it came tilting and groaning over the rough path and broke into the clearing: an electric wheelchair and, seated in it, a dark-haired, bearded man whose powerful upper body was twice the size of his thin, apparently useless legs.

"Shit," I heard Denny say, as the others stared in incredulity from the doorway.

"I told you not to come here!" Denny shouted at the man.

"And since when was it up to you to give me orders, little brother?" the man shouted back.

"Since I was here and you were there," Denny snapped, but at a lesser volume. Then he turned, saying to those gathered in the doorway, "Everybody, this is Jake Lockett, my bullheaded brother. Jake, this is everybody. Now, could you give us a little privacy, please?"

The others shuffled back inside, and Denny closed the door firmly before he dropped from the porch, motioning his brother toward the farthest edge of the clearing—the edge behind which I was barely concealed.

I fought the urge to draw back farther into the inevitably noisy underbrush, hoping they could see less of me than I could of them.

Luckily, they seemed too intent on their encounter to be the least bit aware of their surroundings.

"What possessed you to come here?" Denny demanded.

"You said he was here; where else would I go?"

"There's nothing you can do here," Denny said. "You'll only mess up what I'm into."

"You were here to find him and you did. What is there to mess up?"

"Plenty. I found him, all right, but now he's dead. Murdered."

His brother stared at him. "He was *mine*," he finally hissed.

"He was a lot of people's. And one of them killed him."

"*One of them?*" Jake shot back. "You just couldn't wait, could you? I told you if you confirmed to back off. What did you do, start balling his wife?"

Denny frowned, not meeting his brother's eyes.

"Jesus, you did, didn't you? Is there any woman in the world you *don't* have to have?"

"That had nothing to do with it," Denny said defensively. "That wasn't why he was killed."

"And you know that because . . ."

"Because we didn't do it."

" 'We.' Isn't that cute. I've waited all my life for this

confrontation, and my horny little brother has to add one more notch to his belt. Do you know what that does to . . ." But his voice trailed off as he leaned to see past his brother.

I followed his gaze and saw Amber standing at the far corner of the longhouse. How long, I wondered, had she been standing there?

Denny apparently wondered the same thing and reached for the rear handles of his brother's wheelchair. "We'll go to my tent," he said. "It's not safe to talk here."

"It's not going to be much safer for you there," Jake growled, but fast-forwarded his wheelchair out of his brother's hands and headed in the direction Denny had indicated.

Well, I thought. What am I to make of that?

Answering my next question, Amber turned her head from the men's receding backs and looked straight at my hiding place. My cover, too, had been blown.

I tried to maintain my cool, rising and ambling over to her. "Never a dull moment," I said companionably.

She said nothing, just looked at me with that icy indifference teenage girls seem to have perfected.

"Any idea what that was about?" I said, motioning with my head toward the spot Denny and his brother had just vacated.

She shrugged and looked away.

"Anybody ever tell you you talk too much?"

Her mouth twitched but managed not to smile. Up close it was clear that Amber was well on her way to becoming a beauty. Skinny was turning to slim, sulky to sultry, as her features and her flesh filled in the spaces of her exquisite bone structure. Her small head was topped by a mane of thick, wavy russet hair that almost covered almond-shaped eyes, which were, in fact, amber. I wondered how long she'd had the name and whose idea it had been. From the remote but glamorous pose she was striking, my guess was that it was hers.

"I understand you and Denny used to have a thing," I tried.

That got an answer, complete with eye contact. "It was never a *thing*," she said clearly. "We just fucked."

"Ah." What could you say to that? "Anybody else here interest you?"

Her glance was withering.

"Just fuck 'em and leave 'em, huh?" I said, trying to match her level of ennui.

"What do you want here?" she countered.

Fair enough. "I'm just looking to find out anything I can about Bercain's murder. And the Liberation Brigade," I added, watching her closely for reaction.

Her eyes narrowed slightly and her perfect eyebrows knitted. "That stupid thing," she said scornfully.

"You didn't approve."

"What's the point? So the guy's an asshole. Who isn't?"

"Was everybody involved, or just Denny and his cronies?"

I doubted she'd take that bait, any more than Sam had, and she didn't. But there was interest in her eyes now.

"Is there somewhere we could go and talk," I asked, "without broadcasting our conversation? Frankly, I'd value your take on all this. There don't seem to be too many other level heads around."

That bait she took. And the compliment was genuine enough: I remembered being that age and feeling like an observer among a whole lot of foolish actors. (Before I became a foolish actor myself.)

"The lack of privacy around here must be a drag," I said as I trailed after her around the longhouse, heading away from the main cluster of tents in the direction I'd seen her mother head the morning after the murder. I followed in her wake until she parted the drooping boughs of a cedar to reveal a bright red, dome-shaped tent with a candy-striped awning hung with mosquito netting. A teen-ager's tent.

"So what do you think's going on here?" I asked once I was seated on one of the three red corduroy cushions that filled the half of the tent not occupied by a thick foam pad covered with a green-and-yellow calico quilt. I saw no schoolbooks and wondered whether truancy was another charge the group was leaving itself open to. But I guessed if burglary—not to mention statutory rape—wasn't a concern . . .

Amber shrugged. "Nothing's going on. Just plain nothing."

"Is that nothing interesting or nothing period?"

"They think they're so out there, so big-shot radical. The *Liberation Brigade*? Give me a break. They never even had to break into that house, never stole a thing. She did it all, and they take the credit."

"By 'she' do you mean Kendall Bercain?"

"Yeah, old Kendall baby. Lockett thinks he got some kind of prize. He got nothin' but a gutless rich lady who used him to get back at her husband."

"Did getting back include murder?"

"How would I know?" Amber flipped a thick loop of her hair over her shoulder and swatted the quilt with the flat of her hand. "I can't see Lockett as having the guts to actu-ally kill somebody," she said grudgingly, giving me a flash of eye contact. "He's all talk. You know?"

"Anybody you *can* see as having the guts?"

"Not really. Not anybody around here, anyway. They're all a bunch of losers."

"Does not having enough money to pay your taxes make you a loser?" I said quietly.

She looked at me, surprised, as though I'd gone over to the enemy.

"Is that what happened to your mother?" I asked.

"I guess," she mumbled, staring at the closed flap of the

tent. "I mean, she could have done something herself, you know? She just lived off a man; then when he was gone, she had nothing. Shouldn't have been that dependent in the first place."

"Your father left?"

"Yeah. Fell for some younger chick. It was her own fault: She didn't keep herself up. What did she think would happen? My father was a handsome man."

Amber toyed with the ties on her quilt squares, twisting them one way, then the other.

"How old were you?"

"I dunno," she mumbled. "Nine."

"Do you see your father?"

She shrugged, bit her lower lip to keep it from trembling. "The new one doesn't want me around."

Amber hit the quilt again. "Then this hotshot salesman came along," she said, her eyes blazing. "I couldn't believe it: She actually thought he cared for her. All the man wanted was free bed and board. And me," she added. She looked away.

I waited through the silence that followed.

"But she wouldn't believe *me*," Amber said, more to herself than to me. "She had to see it with her own eyes. By that time it was too late; he'd already gone through her savings and we lost the house. She probably blames me."

"Don't you ever talk about it?"

"What would be the point?" she said glancing at me. "I'm tired of her excuses."

CHAPTER
16

I LEFT THE CAMP even more depressed than when I'd come. Which was going some. Didn't anybody get a childhood anymore?

I slogged along the rutted path, the tracks of Jake's wheelchair already filled by the runoff from the saturated vegetation of the forest floor.

It wasn't until I reached the fairgrounds and crossed toward Sand Run Road that I realized I was heading for Mikah's. But why? If I was looking for an antidote to Amber's story, I could hardly expect to find it at the Horns' dysfunctional fatherless home. So why was I going?

Mikah had touched me, I realized, in ways I didn't fully comprehend. Maybe it was his attachment to his spiritual heritage and his yearning for his father and his Indian ancestry.

Or maybe it was the relationship between the brother and sister, their almost telepathic communion, their reliance on each other. How many such connections were there anymore?

Anymore? Since Scotty—isn't that what I really meant? Scotty had been literally the boy next door, the constant companion of my childhood, then lover in our teens. It had never occurred to me that we would not be together forever. But even that bond had not survived the transition to adulthood. Now my strongest adult relationship was also in peril. How fragile human connections are, I thought, turning north again on Sand Run Road.

My mood didn't begin to lift until the smell of hot cinnamon rolls came drifting from the vents of The Galleon restaurant, making me question my motives for heading in this direction in the first place. I hadn't eaten breakfast, and the aroma turned me faint with hunger. There are times when the best—maybe the only—antidote to pain is a warm cinnamon roll.

It was just after ten o'clock and the restaurant didn't open until eleven, but I pressed my well-known nose to the window, and Eduardo, owner and chef, put down his pan of pastries and came around the counter to the front door to let me in.

"Sugar, sugar, sugar . . ." I panted in only semimock desperation.

Smiling, he returned to the counter and peeled off a piece of the outer ring of one of the huge rolls and popped it into my mouth as I staggered up.

Noting my muddy sweat suit and shoes, Eduardo said, "We don't have a dress code, but maybe we should reconsider."

I made a face in lieu of response.

I ate the rest of the roll standing at the counter talking to Eduardo, then ordered three to go. "I'm going visiting," I said, to explain the number. Of course, I was anticipating sharing with only two others, leaving the third for myself, but he didn't have to know that.

"My best customer," Eduardo said as he handed me the bag and change. "May you always keep running, so you can enjoy my food and still stay as lovely as you are."

I felt definitely less than lovely as I left the restaurant, stepping out into the raw air of a Prince Island winter. I shivered in my damp sweats and broke into a trot the rest of the way to the Horns'.

As I rounded the corner of the alley, I saw Emily sitting in a sandbox at the near end of the apartment complex. She wore a sweatshirt about two sizes too small for her and overalls about as many sizes too large. She didn't look up as I approached, intent upon whatever she was doing. There was no sign of anyone else around, though the children's area—comprised only of the sandbox, a metal jungle gym, and a broken swing—was not enclosed in any way.

"Hi, Emily," I said when I reached her.

She looked up only briefly, without comment, then returned to the skyscraper structure she was building out of objects spread around her, whose sources I shuddered to imagine. Already the tower, based in a weathered boot, had a bit of red print scarf and what looked like the feet of a baby's romper sticking out of the damp sand that was its cement— along with more-treacherous objects such as broken pieces of brown glass and the handle of a pocket knife protruding like guns from a battlement.

"That's quite something you're building," I said to the two-year-old.

She picked up a soup can and jammed it onto the top of the pile, its raggedly cut lid just missing the soft flesh of her other hand.

"Where did you get these things?" I asked, ever hopeful for speech.

She leveled a look at me that let me know she had no intention of answering any questions.

I tried another tack. "Where's Mikah?"

She shook her head, whatever that meant to her.

"Is there anyone at home?"

Again the look.

"I'll just go see," I said, feeling a bit absurd explaining my movements to a small child. Especially one who was not reciprocating.

On the way to the middle building, where the family's apartment was located, I kept an eye out for trash cans, hoping they would appear a reasonable source for Emily's building materials. Seeing nothing on the faces of the three buildings, I walked around to the rear.

There was an overabundance of sources there. In addition to the overflowing Dumpster were dented garbage cans and cardboard cartons full of cans and bottles outside the back door of each building. Must be collection day, I hoped.

By the fourth volley of knocking I had almost concluded that no one was home and was considering calling Social Services, when the door to B-12 was opened by a handsome but bleary-eyed woman in a silky gold dressing gown she held closed at the throat.

"Mrs. Horn?" I said.

Her green eyes narrowed. "What?"

"I'm a friend of your children and I just came by . . ." Why had I come by? "Do you know that Emily is—"

"What's happened? Has she made trouble?"

"No. No. She's just down there by herself and I thought—"

"You from Welfare?"

"No. As I said—"

"A friend."

"Yes. Is Mikah here?"

"No he's not. Why do you think the kid's on her own down there? I can't be watching her every minute. I work nights. I gotta sleep."

At that moment Emily came barreling up the walk and pushed by her mother into the house.

Mrs. Horn seemed about to close the door on me, so I lifted the white bag of cinnamon rolls, saying, "I brought these, on the chance that the kids were at home. They're cinnamon rolls. One for each."

Mrs. Horn waited an unflatteringly long few moments before stepping back from the door so I could enter and did not pause for conversation or even to close the door. She crossed the kitchen to a coffee machine on the littered counter and began measuring brown granules into the pot.

Emily was in the process of clambering into a small high chair she hadn't used the day before. She turned to squeeze her chunky body into the too-tight seat, at the same time trying to pull the tray down over her head. She OD'd on frustration and let loose with a noise like the scolding of crows.

Her mother swung about and glared at her. But Emily was undaunted and hawked again as she managed to cram the tray down over her stomach and began banging on it with both fists in a staccato rhythm.

I figured a peacekeeper was in order and dipped into my bag for a cinnamon roll, which Emily snatched from my outstretched hand and stuffed into her mouth with a gusto worthy of a champion in a pie-eating contest.

The scene spooked me. I'd had little contact with two-year-olds and was vaguely aware that they tended to be strong-willed, pushing the boundaries, but there was something hateful in the way mother and daughter looked at each other. Emily continued to pound on her metal tray while she stuffed one bite of roll after another into her furiously chewing mouth.

I hadn't been invited to sit, but I did, while Mrs. Horn went about making coffee as though neither her tray-banging daughter nor her uninvited guest were present. She'd let loose her grip on the lapels of the dressing gown, and its sleek material swung about her as she moved, revealing a champagne-colored teddy that would have looked ridiculous on me but seemed custom-made for her fuller curves. But although both gown and teddy were of sensuous materials, the effect was anything but sensual. The woman moved in awkward fits and starts that seemed driven by anger. And there were lines at the corners of her mouth and eyes that had not come from laughing. The only element that seemed unaffected by the woman's temperament was a full head of silky, honey-blond hair that must have received its hundred strokes of the brush religiously every night. The effect was of a body at war with itself.

As Mrs. Horn poured a cup of coffee for herself, she said, without turning, "Want some?"

I'm not a coffee drinker but thought it a possible route to congeniality, so I accepted, and she set it in front of me, then dropped into the chair across the table. In turn I passed her a cinnamon roll, using the sack as a plate. The third I simply held in my left hand, feeling more than a little foolish.

"I don't mean to intrude," I said, adding a couple of packets of sugar substitute to the black brew from a bowl in the center of the table. I ripped the second one too vigorously, sending a spray of white grains across the grimy, off-white table. It detracted somewhat from the dignity of the moment, but Mrs. Horn didn't seem to notice.

"I've really enjoyed the company of the children," I began again. "So when Mikah invited me to see his replicas of his father's archaeological finds—"

The woman's head lifted sharply. "You saw those things?"

"Yes. He's very talented," I said, somewhat nonplussed by her tone.

But her gaze had returned to her cup, which she hefted and drained. "He's never let me get near them," she said, but the bitterness of her tone was dulled, like a hurt only vaguely remembered. "Keeps his door locked when he's not here. As though I'd . . ." Her voice trailed off as she stared into the empty cup.

"Mrs. Horn . . ." I began, not sure where I was heading.

"Astrid," she corrected me.

"Astrid. Has Mikah been missing a lot of school?"

Wrong direction. Astrid Horn pinned me with a look that was a grown-up version of Emily's.

"Do you have any idea," she said, emphasizing each word separately, "what it's like to be a single mother raising two children alone?"

I allowed as how I did not.

"Clothes alone," she said. "Even this crummy apartment— a hundred and twenty-eight dollars for electricity alone last month. And this has been a mild winter. Where do you think that money comes from?"

It was a rhetorical question, and she went on. "Your folks probably went to college. But my mother couldn't; she raised me on a lousy secretary's salary. And had to kiss the boss's ass to do it. I swore I'd never get caught like that. But—" She gestured to the room around her. "You married?" she asked.

"No," I said, wincing inside at the turn that made my thoughts take.

"Well, don't," she said flatly. "You think it's going to bring in a paycheck, but it doesn't. Just gives you one more mouth to feed and a whole lot of trouble to get through. Not worth it. Just not worth it."

I figured I hadn't much more to lose by going on. "I understand Mikah's father is in prison," I said, "and you feel it's too far for Mikah to travel alone to visit him."

She stared at me. "The kid must have really spilled his guts to you," she said, "for you to know that." Then she shook her hair, let it settle back on her shoulders with an exhale of coffee-scented breath. "Don't know why he'd want to go. The man doesn't care about him any more'n he ever did about me."

"Well," I said cautiously, "I know he values the letters his father sends—"

Her stare cut me off like a knife through cheese. "Letters? He gets letters, from that slouch?" Her eyes narrowed. "How did you say you know my kid?"

I explained about the making of the luminarias, seeing him again on the beach. "He's an extraordinary boy," I said. "Both the children are."

Astrid shot a skeptical look at her daughter, who was systematically licking icing off her fingers, one at a time. "I don't know what's the matter with her," she muttered. "She just won't talk." Then she bent suddenly toward the high chair. "Not that she's ever *quiet*," she yelled.

Emily returned her mother's look complacently.

"Sometimes I think they're plotting against me," Astrid said through tight lips.

Then I said something I didn't even know was in my mind. "I wonder if I could take him, go with Mikah to visit his father. If that would put your mind more at ease."

The woman's stare swung back to me. "Put my mind at ease?" she repeated with a sort of snort. "If you could do that, young lady, you'd be doing something nobody else ever has. Including me."

CHAPTER
17

THIS WAS GOING TO BE a day of nonstop downers, I thought as I trudged down Sand Run and over Bay Road to Dahlia. Didn't betrayal of innocence used to be the exception rather than the rule? Or had I led too sheltered a life?

Until Chicago, that is, and a rape by someone I thought was a friend. Followed by a year on a big-city police force. That should have cured *anyone* of their illusions. Yet here I was, trying to recover that innocence on an island I thought belonged to a previous era of trust and safety. Even the serial killer I'd encountered in my last case had seemed such an extreme exception, it could hardly be counted.

But who was I kidding? I'd just come from an unhappy look into the lives of three children who weren't being cared for in the manner all children should have a right to expect. Absent fathers, overburdened mothers, a social structure too busy making money to even notice.

Astrid Horn had clearly thought my offer to take Mikah to see his father was motivated by some ulterior, unsavory motive. She had leaned across the kitchen table, her eyes narrowed, and said, "Why would you want to do that? Take off with a *young boy*? Or are you the law trying to take him away from me?"

"No, just a friend," I'd reassured her, hoping I was being fully responsive to her question and that "the law" for her did not include private investigators. I tried to re-member, in fact, whether I'd ever mentioned to Mikah what I did for a living. I didn't think it had ever come up.

At least she'd said she'd think about it. Although giving a hard look at her daughter, she'd added, "I don't know what I'd do with that one, though, if Mikah was away. I can't be here day and night, you know."

I didn't know, and didn't ask, figuring first base was the best I could hope for.

As I climbed the stairs to my office, I went through my usual routine these days, steeling myself to face the an-swering machine. Though I was never sure which would be worse: a blinking light with a devastating message, or no message at all.

The machine was dark. But there was a perfect trigger for my accumulated anger: another of those damn white en-velopes on my floor.

I slammed the door and availed myself of my anger training, cutting loose with some tremendous roars, right from the gut. *Roar* to silence; *roar* to mixed messages; *roar* to the have-nots getting screwed while the haves got fatter; *roar* to families disintegrating from stress and basic unmet needs.

I grabbed the broom from the closet and whacked it against the metal file cabinet, giving off a satisfying *wanggg*. And another. And another. Until between *wangggs* I heard a tentative tap on the door.

I didn't have to wonder who it was: I'd disturbed T-om's meditations again. I opened the door with the apolo-getic look already on my face.

But it wasn't T-om. Kendall Bercain stood there looking definitely apprehensive.

I tried a smile, but it was not returned. "Just blowing off a little steam," I said. (If you can't think of a good lie, try the truth, is my motto.)

She nodded, her face relaxing. "I've broken a few brooms myself," she said, and for the first time I felt some rapport with this woman.

I picked up the envelope from the floor. "Those notes I mentioned? Here's another. Want to see?"

I watched her face closely for any sign that she had already seen the contents of that plain white envelope. I saw none but reminded myself that this woman's face seldom seemed to reveal whatever was going on behind it.

I pulled the white sheet of paper from the envelope. Three words—private NO TrespasSing—the first two cut whole from what looked like magazine pages, the last in four pieces: T, resp, as, and Sing.

I stood frowning at it, then turned to Kendall. "Mean anything to you?"

"Not really," she said, though I thought I saw a flicker of something pass across her eyes.

"Any guesses?"

She shrugged. "I didn't know there was such a thing as privacy anymore."

Good point, I agreed silently.

I waited for her to go on; instead, she seated herself in the client chair, facing the desk, awaiting my occupation of that seat, I supposed.

Usually, I offer a client coffee, which I keep in instant form next to the hot plate, since I don't drink it myself. Or tea, which I do. But my temper tantrum had exhausted me, so I skipped the whole thing and just sat down, without removing my sweaty, grubby windbreaker, the sweats beneath being just as sweaty and grubby. I didn't even offer to take Kendall's crisp taupe raincoat, rationalizing that the woman would probably rather I didn't touch it in my present state.

"The other notes: Did they look like that?" Kendall asked after a few moments of awkward silence.

"Pretty much," I answered, not elaborating.

She sat in silence for another few moments, then seemed to make up her mind and pulled out of her tan leather purse a plain white #10 envelope, and extracted a sheet of white paper, which she rose to slide onto my desk.

NO date at LIGHT house to NIGHT, it read, in various sizes and colors.

Kendall was not making eye contact when I glanced up, so I stood and turned to the windowsill behind me and removed from beneath the water tray of an African violet the key to the *Active* file drawer in the top of my cabinet. From behind the *Bercain* tab in the first hanging file I pulled the folder marked *Notes* and lifted the first four sheets, each paper-clipped to its envelope.

All were 8½ by 11 inches and were thinner than the standard twenty-pound weight of bond. And each seemed to have been pulled from a pad, its top edge slightly rippled, tiny pieces of glue still clinging to it.

I laid them out on my desktop in chronological order, with Kendall's to one side, and motioned for her to come up to look at them. "They appear to have come from the same source," I said. "Same pad, same security-type envelope." I pointed to the blue crosshatching on the inside of each. "When did you receive yours?"

"Sunday," she said. "That's when I was supposed to meet—"

She broke off, so I finished for her. "—Denny at The Second Mate's Lighthouse."

I hadn't looked at her when I said it, to spare her embarrassment. But I turned to her as I asked, "Were you used to sending this sort of note, to arrange rendezvous or whatever?"

"No," she said, flushing. "My schedule has always been pretty much my own. And now that Bercain's gone, there wouldn't be any need for precautions anyway; he could have just called me."

She rubbed her forehead. "Besides which, Denny didn't

seem to know anything about it when I went to break it off with him the next morning. He thought I'd stood him up. I was hurt; I didn't believe him, but now . . ."

"Who all knew about the lighthouse meeting place?" I asked.

"Nobody, I thought," she said. "I obviously wasn't advertising, and so far as I know, Denny wasn't either."

"Would he have told one of the other Squatters? Someone he might be particularly close to?"

"I doubt it," Kendall said. "I think he looks upon the others there as people to lead more than as equals."

Equals. Did that mean that Kendall and/or Denny was class-conscious?

"What is your background, Mrs. Bercain?"

"My background?"

"Yes. Middle class? Old money? New money? No money?"

She shifted her lean, athletic body slightly. "I suppose you could say old money." Then, bitterly, "I'm sure Edmond would never have given me a second look otherwise."

"He didn't come from money?"

"I don't know what he came from, actually," she said, beginning to pace the small room. "He always avoided the subject, except to call himself a 'self-made man.'"

"And Denny?"

She swiveled to look at me, surprised. "Denny? Working class, I suppose, from the way he talked. 'Unions.' 'Organize the workers.' That sort of thing. He seemed to consider himself something of a leftist radical."

"You're using the past tense. Does that mean the affair is over?"

She turned to look out the window, her hands locked together. "I guess," she said finally, her tone stiff as though to keep her emotions in check. "I've probably fulfilled my purpose there too."

I didn't want to probe further in that direction, cause

any more pain, so I moved to the next item. "Whose idea was the poster?"

Kendall gave me another penetrating look. At least, I thought, she knows I'm on the job.

She sighed. "Denny's. And Maia's." She sank back into the client chair, apparently weary of carrying the weight of that little activity.

"Oh, I was enthusiastic," she amended quickly. "I was thrilled to expose the man for the two-faced ass he was. When Denny proposed it, I couldn't have been more accommodating."

"Including burgling your own possessions?"

Kendall made a dismissive gesture. "I don't care about that stuff. The grounds, yes; the possessions, no. I'm not your basic furs-and-diamonds rich lady, never have been." For the second time that afternoon she reached into her bag and extracted a cigarette, then appeared to remember where she was and put it back.

I was surprised to hear myself say, "It's okay if you want to smoke." I could open the window after she left, I thought.

She gave me a grateful look and lit up—with a matchbook rather than a lighter, true to her self-description of indifference to money.

"I guess I never had that period of rebellion most kids have," she said at the tail end of a long exhale of smoke. "My biggest rebel act was to wear jeans instead of the color-coordinated little outfits my mother brought back from her shopping sprees."

I reached into my desk drawer for a cigarette from a pack a client had left and carried it with me to the client chair. I wanted a look at that matchbook.

Kendall raised it to strike me a light. Its cover was shiny white, without lettering, only the figure of a bird in raised gold on the upper left-hand corner.

She took a drag of her own. "Luckily," she said sarcastically, "she didn't notice me enough to make much fuss. And my father was too busy piling up the bucks to be there."

As I reseated myself, Kendall gave me an ironic look, heavy with old pain. "And then they died. My father's latest toy plane went down on the way to Tahoe. Now you see 'em, now you don't."

"Rough," I said.

She shrugged and smoked contemplatively for a few moments, while I went through the motions and tried to keep from choking. Then she stretched her neck and flexed her shoulders, as though bringing herself back to the present. "So when Denny suggested playing Robin Hood with some of the more conspicuously consumptive items in that house, I thought it was a hoot. And how much legal noise could Bercain make without exposing the fact that absolutely none of it was his?"

A rare smile curved her wide, lipstickless mouth and then was gone, leaving the sculpted bone structure of her face looking gaunt and tired.

"Who all was involved?" I asked her.

She gave me a guarded look, which prompted me to add, "My client has no interest in prosecuting the matter, and my only obligation regarding her own premises and possessions is to her."

She smiled again and said, "Sam and Iris. Frank and Leonard. Amber." Kendall blew out a huff of smoke. "She really got into it. Fancied herself a Bonnie to Denny's Clyde, apparently. Of course, it took me a while to figure that out. But then, why would I think a fifteen-year-old would be off-limits for the great Romeo of the Forest?"

I tried to get my client back on track. "Did the rest of the group know about the plan? Even those who didn't participate?"

"I assume so. Dorothy didn't approve, of course. But

then, she doesn't approve of much. And Maia was all for the posting but not the stealing. Not a part of her Moral Code." Her tone capitalized the last two words.

"Would either Maia or Dorothy have told anyone? Involved anybody else?"

Kendall shook her head. "I doubt it. Maia was intent on her own complaints. And I doubt Dorothy had anybody to tell; keeping Amber in check seemed to be her full-time job." She took a puff, then added, "Really, though, I don't think any of them would have killed the man. Pranks were more their style."

"Interesting," I said slowly. "Your husband called them 'pranks' as well." I was stalling for time while I tried to decide whether to tell Kendall that Denny might have more "complaints" than she knew. Unless maybe she did know.

"Did Denny ever mention a brother?" I asked.

She thought a moment, shook her head. "I don't think so."

"Did he talk about his family at all?"

Kendall's color rose a shade. "Actually, we didn't do all that much talking when we were together. But when I was at the camp, I never heard him mention any."

"Were you at the camp before you got involved with him romantically?"

"No," she said grimly. "The sex was the hook."

I decided to leave it at that until I could explore the subject further on my own.

"What do you know about your husband's business contacts?"

"Nothing," she said flatly. "He never brought his business home. At least not to me," she added, and crushed out her cigarette in the saucer I'd given her. "I don't think he found me presentable enough to be taken out in public much. And I certainly had no desire to rub elbows with that lot."

"He never brought anyone home? To dinner or whatever?"

"Only Earl Moulton, his campaign manager. I think he was taking my measure as a potential mayor's wife. Not to mention a governor's."

"How did it go?"

Kendall gave a small smile. "I put on a dress, if that counts."

"But personally?"

She frowned, was silent a moment. "I'm not sure I consider the political animal a person. Feed in the party line, the latest poll, out it spews from its mouth. Bercain's opinions could take a hundred-eighty-degree turn overnight, depending on what anybody 'important' wanted to hear."

I smiled. "How much are you exaggerating?"

She smiled back. "Not much. It seemed to be part of the 'self-made' syndrome. I never saw anybody so eager to please 'the right people.' I guess I was part of that effort. Not a very effective part, but I guess you get what you pay for."

"What did you get out of the deal?"

Kendall's high forehead furrowed. "At first? The fairy-tale wedding, the handsome groom." She stood, lit another cigarette, began pacing again. "I wish I could say those things never mattered to me." She shrugged. "But, hey, I may not be your standard Barbie doll, but I am an all-American girl; I got fed the same diet of romantic trash."

She threw me a wry look. "But did I learn my lesson? Nope. After Ken comes Ken Junior. Only the wardrobe changed. But li'l Barbie hopped right back on the bandwagon." She rolled her eyes, adding, "To mix a metaphor."

I was beginning to like this woman; she seemed to be the real thing. And her apparent reticence made me wonder what friends she had that she could open up to. Which opened a cavity in my own heart. With the absence of Free and Gray, I felt the loss of my own intimate connections.

Maybe one best friend and one lover–best friend were too few, too easy to lose and be left with no one. Even as independent as I prided myself on being, two minus two equaled zero.

I stirred myself from my thoughts and said, "What do you know about your husband's dealings with Maia, which ended in his owning her business and closing the shop?"

"Not much. But what Maia said about it at the camp didn't surprise me. I don't think Bercain ever thought twice about ethics. Principles versus pragmatism: If it worked, it was good. And if it made money, it worked. Period."

She stubbed out her cigarette and resumed pacing. "But isn't that what 'successful' people do?" Her fingers had described quote marks in the air around the word *successful* and continued to mark others. "He thought me too naive for words and threw my money at me—my 'shield' from the compromises 'real life' requires." The frown lines returned. "Hell, for all I know, he was right. He's sure got lots of company."

She'd set her ashtray on top of the file cabinet and now propped her elbow there as well, bent her forehead to her palm.

I waited a decent interval before I probed another probably painful area. "If the marriage was pretty much over, were there any other women in his life?"

The swiftness with which Kendall's head rose gave me my answer there. "Many, I'm sure," she said shortly.

"Do you know of anyone in particular?"

"You mean whom I've seen him with or just seen their chummy pictures in the paper?"

I'd already covered the latter group. "Seen him with, I guess."

A muscle along her jaw began working. "Well, besides Betty and Marion, I saw him with a blonde once I'd never seen before. And I do mean *blonde*. Pure platinum. At The Queen's Rest."

I knew the place from my last big case: a fancy restaurant on a bluff overlooking Angelina Bay. Much frequented by off-islanders, I'd heard, and by natives not wanting to be seen together.

"I don't go out much," Kendall continued. "Especially to restaurants alone. But this once I'd decided to treat myself to a non-Latino lunch. The sun was shining for a change, and I heard The Queen had good lobster."

She lit another cigarette. "When I saw them, at some candlelit table in the rear, I remember thinking that the woman looked like a whore in expensive business clothes. I left immediately and never went back."

"When was that?"

She was shielding her face again. "Maybe a year ago, a little less."

"Was that the only time you saw them together?"

She nodded. "But it was about that time he started staying out later and later. Then overnight a few times."

"And you have no idea who she was?"

"Nope," Kendall said. "And I didn't try to find out. He wasn't in my bed, so why should I care who else's he was in? Let him turn on them too."

At that moment there were a rapid few raps on the door, it opened, and Her Honor the Mayor stuck her head in, singsonging, "Knock-knock."

You know how there are some people—women mostly, I'm afraid—who never seem to close their mouths completely? It's the wide-open-mouth smile, and it just never seems to shut between conversation deliveries. Maid Marion is one of those.

It seemed especially wide that day.

"I heard you were looking for me?" she said, as though she were offering a child a treat.

I saw Kendall's face freeze, though she was hidden from Marion behind the door.

"Yes," I said, my gaze traveling between the two

women. "I'm investigating Mr. Bercain's death. For his wife here."

Marion's cherry-red smile also froze, and Kendall stepped out into view. "Mayor," she said coldly.

The look on Marion's face told me two things: one, that she had indeed been having an affair with Edmond Bercain, and two, that she knew Kendall was aware of it.

But Kendall cut the confrontation short. "I must be going," she said to me briskly. "Keep me informed." And she scooped up her purse from the client chair and was gone.

"Poor woman," Marion murmured at the closed door. "She must be lost without Edmond. I don't think she ever goes out without him. Just putters around in that garden of hers. Such a strange woman for a man of business to marry, don't you think?"

But she didn't wait for an answer, just crossed to the client chair and lowered her perfect size-eight body into it. "I thought I'd just come see what you wanted," she said, recovering the dazzling smile. "I just got back from dropping my daughter at the U-Dub." (Local-speak for the University of Washington.)

"I swear," she said, leaning back with decorous exhaustion, "I don't know where this past year has gone. Already she's into her second semester. Can you imagine?"

"Ms. Stephenson-Roth—"

"Oh, Marion, please."

"Marion. Did you see Mr. Bercain at all on the thirty-first?"

"Actually, yes, I did. I knew he was out of town, but after I saw that terrible poster I called him at Mr. Moulton's. That's where he was—*they* were—staying, in Monterey. Mr. Moulton had recently become his campaign manager, you know. A brilliant man. I'm sure that with his help Edmond could have become a wonderful successor to me when I have to step down next fall."

She moved her hand to her head, smoothing her perfectly smooth cap of honey-brown hair. "Edmond came by the shop that next morning. He said, in fact, that he was on his way to see you, to see what you might find out about the posters. He suspected the Squatters, of course. Just what you'd expect from such an irresponsible . . . gang."

"So he said. Did you see him at all after that morning? In the evening, for instance?"

"Why, no. I was at the shop all day, and then . . . Well, you know, Hugh and I had to go to the school to see those little lights the kids had made."

She turned on the smile again. "That was so wonderful of you to work with those . . . difficult children. And then to set the lights out along the parade route for us too. . . . Really, you were an invaluable help. I wonder that you no longer work in theater."

"I have my hands full here," I mumbled. "So you didn't see him at all later, during the parade perhaps?"

"Oh, my goodness! I was so frantically busy, I didn't even *look* at anybody. I love costume events, don't you? Trying to guess who everybody is? But we'd agreed to take some children out for the parade. From that wonderful Sister Teresa House in Port Angel. They take children waiting to be placed in foster care, you know, and they are so in need of a little entertainment while they're in transition like that. So Alan and I—"

She put her hand over her mouth, though her eyes were still gleaming with mirth. "Oops." She leaned forward then and whispered, "If you can keep a secret, I'll tell you that Alan Gartrell and I have been keeping company since he and Sandy decided on divorce. We try to be discreet, since most people aren't aware of their plans. I know when I was going through my divorce—"

She shook herself, of all unpleasant thoughts apparently. "Anyway, we thought the costume parade would be a perfect way to go out in public without embarrassing

Sandy. So then when the House called me, asked if I could take those poor little children to the parade, of course I had to say yes. They said they had these mouse costumes, so perhaps I could go as the Pied Piper. But we already had our costumes. With his mustache and that gorgeous olive skin, Alan was a natural for an organ grinder. He even had this accordion he used to play in grade school! So he wanted to go as an organ grinder, which made me just have to be his little monkey. Isn't that a hoot!"

I was beginning to wonder whether the woman ever stopped for breath.

"Anyway, we went and got them. . . . Then they got scared of the parade—all that crowd, and the strange costumes—I don't know what those Teresa people could have been thinking. And nothing would calm those kids down. Not ice cream, not riding on his shoulders. . . . So Alan and I just had to take them back. That was about ten. And by the time that staff had stopped bending our ear—couldn't the bank help with funding; couldn't we hold a fund-raiser here in Grace—we missed the whole New Year's gala. Not so much as a whistle at midnight."

The woman sat back again—as exhausted as I was, maybe, by her performance. "So I didn't see Edmond at all. I'd be surprised if he even went to the parade, as upset as he was. He could be very moody, you know. And he couldn't take his wife; she'd never go to such a fun event. I told the police the same thing. They checked. Alan and I weren't even in town during the time poor Edmond was killed."

If her tactic had been to wear me down so I wouldn't question her further, she had done a good job. Both their alibis would be easy to check.

"Well," I said, "thank you, Marion. If you've nothing more to tell me, I'll let you go. I'm sure you're very busy."

"You have no idea!" she said as I opened the door for

her. "I'm telling you, I am going to be one relieved lady when this term as mayor is up. Four years is just too many for this load of responsibility. I'm going to be so glad to have *me* time again."

"I'm sure you will," I said, and closed the door after her.

CHAPTER
18

By the time the door closed behind Mayor Maid Marion, if I never spoke to another person, it would be too soon.

I wasn't crazy about sitting around next to the phone either. And the only thing I'd had to eat that day were two monster sweet rolls.

I locked the door and crept down the stairway carefully, so as not to arouse T-om or Eugene in their lairs, and made it out the door into murky gray air that exactly mirrored my mood. Not even the bay was visible, let alone Mount Baker beyond.

I had almost reached The Blue Heron when I spotted Alan Gartrell step from his silver-gray BMW at the curb several cars down and wave to a woman in Marion S-R's pink pantsuit standing in the doorway of The Heron.

Quickly, I crossed the street and backtracked on Nutmeg and turned north.

I made it all the way to the beach without having to more than nod at another person and broke into a run. How many miles did this make today, I wondered. Two plus four plus three or so . . . Maybe I'd just sleep in the office tonight. And burn these clothes tomorrow.

I did not stop at The Faces. (There was some sense to be

made of life? Get real.) And I pounded on past the PRIVATE NO TRESPASSING sign without breaking stride, my thick soles slapping the sand.

I had made it as close to the bay marina as I wanted to get and had turned back, when suddenly the beach up ahead of me was flooded with a white glare.

I looked up. The spotlights around the big white house I'd seen before on the cliff were staring down like monster grasshoppers that had just spied a juicy crop. The lights were so strong, I could barely see the fresh white paint on the house behind them.

WHITEHOUSE.

Even a LIGHTHOUSE now, in a way.

And just below it on the beach, a PRIVATE NO TRES-PASSING sign.

I shook myself like a dog shedding water. Get a grip, I said silently; not all big white houses that forbid trespassing signal TWISTED TIMES or FALSE LOVE. Even TRUTH IN ADVERTISING.

Still . . .

I moved toward the escarpment, trying to shield my eyes from the glare and get a better sense of the layout of the property above. The high, fat deck I'd noticed before wrapped the southern third of the house. And from the northern corner of its sheer face, I could just make out the peaks of a white picket fence—but higher than the cottage variety, tall enough to cover any windows on that side of the house.

I closed my eyes, bright pinpoints from the spotlights dancing across the darkness of my lids. Those spots would prevent most scrutiny from outsiders, I thought. Something to hide.

Suddenly, getting a closer look at that house was an overwhelming desire. I started at a faster run back toward the stairway.

———

Sunflower Street is the exception to the east-west-herbs, north-south-flowers pattern of streets in Grace. A continuation of Parsley from the library, it curves around the higher face of the bluff, all the way to the bay. The properties on its western side are highly valued for their unobstructed views of the water, but—until now, apparently—the face of the escarpment was thought too risky to build on. Too steep and subject to slides. More coins had pressed palms, apparently.

I trotted south along Sunflower, looking for the sign down on the beach that would signal the new ediface above. And a driveway on my left, unless the occupants helicoptered in.

I might have missed the narrow gravel drive altogether had there not been a duplicate of the sign below posted at its mouth: PRIVATE NO TRESPASSING. And at a sharp curve some thirty feet beyond, another that said PRIVATE DRIVE. Exclusivity in triplicate.

Even from the drive, though, the house was invisible below, the steep slope and outcroppings of boulders shielding it from view.

My stakeout alert came on. I *really* wanted to see who came and went on that driveway over the course of an evening. The overlit house looked for all the world as though it were expecting company. Just none that would breach its well-posted privacy.

Already dusk was coming on, further darkening the prematurely dim sky that had apparently triggered the lights to go on early. I would have just enough time before dark to fuel up the ol' body before it would be time to post myself nearby. I'd have to take a cab home anyway since I'd been on foot all day; it might as well be later as sooner. Maybe I'd even be worn out enough by then to sleep. Though I wasn't going to count on it.

I picked up a cold Philly sub at The Market on Parsley, along with a carton of orange juice for my stressed immune system, and returned to my office to add long johns to my muddy outfit.

The answering machine was still dark.

I left the office munching the sandwich and downing the juice, crossed on Sage to Rose and down to Sunflower. There was a house on that corner I knew, which had a dense hedge along the sidewalk. The owners, Fred and Claire Stocking, were "snowbirds"—those who fly south for the winter. But they'd given Free several starts from the *rosa rugosas* that formed their hedge, semiwild roses that thrive on sea salt. Even in winter the bushes would be dense and studded with orange-red hips.

I cut across the Stockings' side lawn to position myself behind the hedge and was satisfied with the view it gave me of the street and driveway. Both were visible thanks to the lights from the house below.

It had been three-quarters of an hour, and I was getting impatient, when a taxi coming south along Sunflower stopped at the drive and a woman in a red cape and high heels got out.

It wasn't until she straightened and the light glinted off her thick russet hair that I recognized her: Amber.

As the taxi started up again, she stooped, removing one fire-engine-red heel, then the other. And when the taxi disappeared up Rose, she turned and began walking down the loose-gravel drive, holding the shoes in one hand.

I began to move forward on the other side of the hedge, telling myself it couldn't be the way it looked, when a spanking new white Corvette came speeding up Sunflower and barely made the turn into the drive, spraying gravel in a wide arc.

I had gotten a glimpse of the driver as it passed: a woman, with bright platinum hair.

After that there was no way I wasn't going down there.

I waited what felt like an eternity until another car—this one middle-aged and traveling slower—turned down the drive. Then I crossed the street and began the descent myself.

There were two more twists of the narrow drive after the first, skirting boulders, before the house appeared below me—or as much as I could make out of it with the glare of spotlights in my eyes. The floodlights in front were trained on the beach below, but there were two others in the back trained upward, toward the drive and street. Clearly, none of the lights were there to aid visibility but to produce a high-wattage *in*visibility.

From what I could see, my hand shielding my eyes, the picket fence I had glimpsed from below rose at least ten feet around the house, making any windows there might be in the rear wall well-hidden. *Fortress* was the word that came to mind, however elegant its architecture.

I moved carefully on down the slippery gravel, until the sound of another motor—this one critically rough—sent me to the shadows of an outcropping of rocks.

When I heard the motor stop, I chanced a peek between boulders and saw the driver of that car emerge in a clingy sequined blue gown. She proceeded to a gate in the fence and made a gesture like the passing of a card down the groove of an ATM machine.

The gate swung slowly open, and the woman went through, the glitter of her spotlighted gown seeming to linger as the gate ground closed behind her.

From this vantage point I could see that there were two graveled areas, one to either side of the drive. To the left sat the two aging cars, while the white Corvette sat alone to the right.

Below me, I saw no cover among the smaller boulders, so I decided to stay where I was for the time being, in case there were more cars to come.

Over the next half hour three more modest vehicles joined those on the left, and their female drivers also passed through the gate.

Then the fancy cars began to arrive. I counted three Lincolns; two shiny BMWs, one black, one silver-gray; and two white Cadillacs—all with male drivers, parking on the right.

Then, just as I was about to chance it on the drive again, another car tore past—one that looked lucky to be running at all—and braked to a stop in the left-hand lot.

The driver slammed the car door hard and strode toward the gate like a tiger on the prowl, her tawny blond hair rippling about her shoulders.

I couldn't even see her face, but I was certain of it: Astrid Horn.

She seemed to be having trouble with her card, jamming it down, then pulling it free with a curse I could hear even from where I sat, then jamming it down again. It struck me that mother and daughter might not be all that unalike after all.

Then my butt and boredom had all of waiting on a cold hard stone they could take, and I scuttled down the slope, jumped to the gravel lot, and took off around the corner of the picket fence, until I couldn't be seen from the driveway.

At least now I was beneath the angle of the spotlights and could look around me.

The picket fence wrapped the back half of the house completely until the deck took over, about three feet higher, at the far end. I imagined myself tripping over the tops of those pickets and leaping to the deck, but I decided that would take more of an aerialist than a gymnast and looked for Plan B.

Only a narrow dirt path separated the fence from the rocky cliff behind it. My leg and back muscles began to rehearse how I might brace myself against that cliff and literally climb the fence in a semihorizontal position. Maybe if I could get over the fence, there would be windows I could see through and ways to get up on that deck with access to the second story.

I'd seen a rope holding shut the passenger door of Astrid Horn's semblance of a car, and that seemed a possible third element in such a plan.

I backtracked to the battered blue car and pried at the stubborn knots at both bumpers that held the rope in place over its bent door, glancing over my shoulder every other moment. The soggy knots finally loosened and I made it back behind the fence just in time to avoid being spotted by a red Jaguar that took the twists in the gravel drive like a race car at the Indy 500. (Not that I've ever seen the Indy 500.)

The pickets looked questionably strong enough to bear my weight, so I studied the position of the top crosspiece to which the pickets were nailed. If I could loop the rope around that two-by-four . . .

I tied a knot in one end and tossed it over the fence, succeeding in passing it between the two chosen pickets with my first throw—one of the skills I'd retained from the Western phase of my early childhood, when I'd fancied myself a cowgirl extraordinaire, destined for a movie career of derring-do at the very least. I could still remember the passion with which I'd yearned for a pony. Still wouldn't turn one down, in fact. And though a horse would be more fitting to my years, let's face it: A pony would still do for size.

Getting the rope back through those same two pickets proved harder. Starting it swinging front to back instead of side to side seemed to require a longer arm than I had on hand (as it were), and I had to find a thin, long stick to help me. Then I had to snag its forked end around the rope below the crosspiece and twist it to hold. I was getting mightily frustrated before I finally hooked the rope securely and pulled, snatching the knotted end with my left hand at the last minute before it could swing back again.

I made a slipknot and tightened it to the upper bar, then tied the other end around my waist. After all, I reflected, the rope would provide something of a safety net—more than I'd ever had in a gym.

I began with my butt on the boulder behind me and my feet flat on the fence, then lifted myself by the rope to see whether it would hold my ninety-seven pounds.

It held, so far. So I began to pull, hand over hand, my knees bent, my feet inching upward.

This was definitely harder than I'd rehearsed it in my mind. Even with the maximum tread of the new running shoes I'd bought myself for Christmas, it was torturous going, and the rough rock surface at my back was taking its toll.

When I ran out of rock, though, it was harder. Luckily, I reached the lower horizontal bar soon after and was able to rest, deadweight against my extended arms, my feet on the bar, wedged between the pickets.

Then I started up again, by now stiff-armed and stiff-legged but shortening my hold on the rope as I neared the top so I'd be within reach of the picket points when I got there.

This did, of course, give me less traction as my shoes' contact with the fence lessened, and my feet slipped more than once before I was finally able to grab the top of a picket with my right hand and hoist the left knee to the upper horizontal bar. Thus precariously braced, I peered over the pointed peaks of the fence, my left hand trying to shield my eyes from the floodlights, their beams now flowing about two feet over my head toward the road above.

If I'd expected S&M scenes and dancing girls, however, there were none in sight—at least from my perch. Beyond the cold bare dirt of a non-yard, there was a series of floor-to-ceiling windows all across the back of the house. Strange architecture if you had something to hide. Hence the fence, I supposed.

Unfortunately, all the windows were fully draped, in some opaque mahogany-brown fabric. Only the window at the far end of the house gave any glimpse of the interior. Through an opening in the drapes only a few feet wide, the scene beyond shimmered in the soft glow of candlelight.

Along the right edge of the gap was a slice of what looked to be a black marble fireplace, though there was no fire in it and no chimney above it on the roof. One of the two men standing next to it, however, was finding its mantel a handy resting place for his forearm and the wineglass his hand was toying with. The man was tall, with a generous shock of white hair and a large nose—a face I recognized from my newspaper search as that of Earl Moulton, Bercain's campaign manager.

The other was Alan Gartrell.

Both wore well-tailored suits, but they were easily outshone by the glittering white gown of the person facing them—a tall, runway-thin woman with a stylish upsweep of platinum-blond hair.

Could it be, I thought, chagrined to be disappointed, that the only thing going on here was your standard stuffy cocktail party?

I didn't so much decide to climb back down as my wedged knee and my grip on the peak of the fence began to slip their hold and let gravity have its way with me.

It was faster going down than up, by a good deal, and my extensive vocabulary of gutter talk got a workout, though I swallowed most of it in case anybody was within hearing range.

I sat where I had dropped, trying to decide whether I had learned my lesson now or was determined to risk life and limb again to get a closer look at whatever was going on in the second story of that house.

Walk away? That'd be new.

Besides, this brilliantly lit mansion had become a kind of nose-thumbing symbol to me, perched on its peak, shielded by laws of privacy, flaunting whatever was going on there, legal or not. Already I'd seen two women I cared about—one a mere girl—go into that fortress dressed like call girls, who from the looks of their rides weren't even getting much of the pot. I was going to find out just what they were being expected to do there.

So I hauled my bruised body up, tried and failed to release the rope from the fence, and continued without it down the narrow path toward where the sweep of the deck began above.

From where I then stood at the eastern corner of the house, I could see wide French doors separating the second floor from the deck and, behind them, soft flickering lights. More candles. Could it be, I thought again, that there was no more going on above than there seemed to be downstairs?

Then I remembered Amber's spike heels. And her age. A teenager was unlikely, after all, to be sought out for the clever repartee she could offer to a cocktail gathering of middle-aged businessmen. And conversation was unlikely to be their objective anyway. There was only one thing men seemed to value in a beautiful sixteen-year-old. And she surely did have that. And probably had learned how to use it.

Cynic, I grumbled to myself as I eyed the tall supports of the deck above. Not scalable that I could see, even if I still had the rope. There had to be a better way.

I studied the terrain. The house had been built on a natural shelf in the formation of the cliff, which dropped sharply from its face, as though the structure had fought its way to the front of some line. There was barely room on the western side for the two small parking lots, and the cliff wrapped tight to the house's rear. But at the eastern end the gray crags and boulders rose in more irregular formations, with scraps of brush tucked into their bends and pockets. Even a few small wind-bowed trees hung on by their roots among the boulders.

One such tree leaned toward the house from a ledge about five feet on a diagonal above the deck. I narrowed my eyes at its lowest branch, gauging the line of sight it would afford of the second-story interior through those French doors.

The limbs of the crooked tree were bare of leaves. But so were all deciduous trees in the month of January. That didn't mean it was—for instance—dead. It could just as likely be alive.

The only way to know would be to test it, I reasoned, already scrambling up the rocks in as direct a route to the tree as the terrain allowed, climbing toehold to handhold in the white light from the defending floodlights. At least, I noted as the wicked thorns of a bush with red berries warned my right hand not to come nearer, most of the lights at this eastern end of the house were trained above the rocks. Toward future neighbors, should another builder have this much clout with the powers that be? Only the two end spots and one in the middle were angled straight out. Three out of nine; the odds could be worse.

I made it to the tree with only minor scrapes and bumps and pushed at the foot-wide trunk, as though its resistance would be a reliable proof of the state of its health. It was, at least, no pushover, so I put it to the second test of my weight, jumping for the lowest branch.

The branch held—and, as importantly, bent—so I continued to climb. About twice my body height farther, I was able to touch the branch I was aiming for. Getting there, however, would be harder, as there were no branches or even footholds between it and the one on which I stood.

I hadn't done chin-ups in a while, and they proved less effortless than I remembered, but I pulled, then pushed, then clambered, until I made it, straddling the branch.

I sat, my hand against the trunk, resting and congratulating myself. Until I turned toward the deck and realized that the central spotlight, the one aimed horizontally from the roof, hit me straight in the face, its glare all but blinding my sight.

I held up a hand as shield and was able to deflect the

beam enough to make out the French doors. But my perch was too high to see through them, even if the spotlight would permit, which it would not.

I was going to have to jump to the deck.

Even before my gymnastics years I had pushed my ability to climb, jump, and survive a fall, in my friendly rivalry with Scotty, my constant companion in the woods near our homes. Indifference to pain, I had discovered, was a necessary ingredient of success. The virtually certain byproducts—minor bruises and abrasions, or worse—simply could not be a part of the conscious mind when engaged in risky activities.

Acting on that principle, not to mention my insatiable curiosity, I stood, still balanced against the trunk, and looked with shielded eyes from my limb to the deck.

Okay, it was possible. Probably.

I rehearsed in my mind and muscles the necessary maneuvers: the grip, the swing, the launch—to what height— the full somersault for extra reach and velocity, then the grab for the rail—at which point I should be beneath the spotlight's beam and able to see in. Right? Right.

With no small children to provide for, apparently, the space between the shoulder-high rail and the deck was wide open. And while it would not be enough for even *my* legs to swing under at full length, they should be able to pass through if raised to the height of my hips.

Nerves do not improve with hesitation, so after one more mental run-through I swung off from my limb for the deck.

I understood early, working out on the uneven bars, why the Wright brothers kept at it till they got it right. Flying feels every bit as natural as running—and more thrilling—once the mind trusts the body's abilities. Only one other trick of the muscles comes close to the intense magic of that sensation.

At least the airborne part.

The right leg made it through under the rail; the left did not, its inner thigh slamming against the sharp edge of the deck, possibly jeopardizing my participation in the afore-mentioned magic forever and leaving me hanging half on, half off, with a full view of my alternative landing place on the rocks below.

Definitely not a 10, I groaned inwardly as I hauled the left leg up and under. Unless you count the survival factor.

I lay flat on my back, discreetly stifling my groans, as I watched the beam of the middle spotlight make a mini-Milky Way of the swath of air above my head. Lulling strains of elevator music seemed to be a part of the show, and my lids grew heavy, my body begging for rest. Until I re-membered that music meant activity, and it was the interior show for which I'd come all this way.

I roused myself to all fours, ignoring the pain that now pervaded my body. The music was coming from beyond the French doors, across the deck on my right, so I crawled toward them, keeping to one side of their glass and staying low.

Once at the wall, I flattened myself to the deck floor again, this time on my stomach. The boards smelled strongly of fresh varnish, its pungency overpowering the saltwater scent of the air. But I was thankful that at least I wouldn't be adding splinters to my other wounds as I snaked my way to the ledge of the glass doors.

The scene within was in some ways what I'd expected, in others, not. Sex for hire did seem to be on the program, but most of the actual contact I saw was between three pairs of naked women on a raised hexagonal platform. There were three mattress-size dips in the platform's surface, on which the women lounged, caressing themselves and each other with all the passion of applying suntan lotion.

Around the platform were arranged club chairs covered in red plush. All their occupants were male, fully clothed ex-cept for a few open zippers. Some were visibly responding, some with the aid of the women who were still gowned.

Amber was one of those center stage. She was paired with a woman considerably older, whose gaze was fixed on Amber's perfect young body as though it were cake and she'd been dieting for years.

Amber, on the other hand, wore a smile that was one part amusement and three parts contempt. She looked indifferent not only to her partner but to everyone in the room.

The Muzak-type sound system began playing "Love Is a Many-Splendored Thing," which must have been a cue, because the women switched to self-stimulation.

I felt the same bafflement I had at the age of twelve when I'd run across issues of *Playboy* in Scotty's closet. It seemed that all the well-endowed bodies on its pages were engaged in one form or another of masturbation, a skill I'd just learned. "I'd think that would make you feel left out," I'd said to Scotty then. "If they can do it themselves, what do they need you for?"

But maybe that was the point, I thought now: safe, remote pseudosex, seeking only the vicarious sensation of the moment. The whole scene was profoundly depressing.

I was almost relieved when a door opened on the eastern wall of the room and a man entered arm in arm with one of the women I'd seen pass through the front gate. She walked with him to a door at the northern edge of the room, where he slipped something into her hand and left.

The oldest profession the old-fashioned way, I thought. A poor replacement for love, but at least contact. I wondered whether the bill the woman had apparently been slipped was full payment or just a tip. The difference between self-employment and even greater exploitation: the pimp/madam pocketing most of the hard-earned—*very* hard-earned—money.

Then, as though called to the stage by my thoughts, the door opened again and the platinum blonde glided through, ushering in two men I hadn't seen before, less elegantly dressed than Moulton or Gartrell but clearly prosperous.

She walked casually around the perimeter of the room, one man on each side, gesturing alternately toward the doors on her left and the scene in the center, as though making a presentation.

Potential investors? Had Bercain been one of those investors, interested less in a mistress than in an addition to his fortune? Or business *and* pleasure? Or had they both joined what seemed to be a growing number of people for whom business had become the *greatest* pleasure?

I was jolted from my thoughts by the progression of the trio—not around to the other side of the room as I'd expected but toward the doors through which I was gazing from the deck floor. It seemed that my assumption that the deck would not be used in winter had to be added to all my other assumptions that had proved false.

I looked frantically about for a place to hide and found none. It would have to be over the edge.

I hunched like an inchworm, quickly pulling back from the doors toward the western edge of the deck, turning only just in time to keep from backing off it altogether.

I looked down and scooted over so my legs were aligned with one of the posts supporting the deck. No time to worry that my legs were too short to wrap fully around it; I simply grabbed the railing and slithered under it, wrapping legs, then arms, like a koala bear about the sharp square post below.

As the door opened I heard a man's voice say, "At least take my jacket."

"Thank you, Mr. Watts."

"Franklin."

"Franklin."

Then gravity took over, and I began a slide that ended in an abrupt, spine-jangling encounter with the dirt below.

I didn't dare move from the ungraceful position my limbs had landed in, as I heard the other man's voice say, "You're right, it's a magnificent view."

Then the woman's voice. "The success of Love's Throne has been greater than we even projected at this stage of the investment."

"I still wonder about security. As exposed as it is."

"Hidden in plain sight, as they say. The lights and the terrain provide a substantial barrier. And of course none of the paperwork identifies our investors, any more than it does our clientele."

Then I heard the door open again, and the woman's voice said, "What is it, Astrid?"

"I wonder if I could leave early. My daughter's sick, one of her fevers. I left her with her brother, but . . ."

"I guess we're adequately covered. Be sure to write down your hours."

I didn't move until the cold finally drove the three back indoors; then instantly I scrambled from under the deck, back to the path, and around behind the fence.

I had just reached the stuck rope when I heard Astrid Horn's car belch to life, and saw it grind—now ropeless— up the bumpy gravel drive.

"Sorry," I said to it, for more than just the rope.

I took off up the drive myself and made it onto Sunflower, limping north to find a taxi.

Then I saw the gleam of headlights go on behind me and heard the silky purr of a car's engine igniting. I lowered my head, my hands to my nose as though sneezing into a tissue as the car glided toward me up Sunflower, then turned left onto Lily. Peeping over my hands, I could almost swear that the car was a forest-green Lexus.

CHAPTER
19

As the taxi turned into Free's drive, I thought I saw a glimmer of light in the bedroom of her cottage. Just a reflection of the headlights, I told myself, trying to wake up from the catnap I'd taken during the brief ride.

The cab pulled up behind my car and I handed the driver about twice what I owed him, so grateful that this, at least, was one leg of the day's circle I hadn't had to walk.

I'm a homebody of sorts: I love my own bed, with its wraparound view of the woods, all the fragrances drifting in through the camper's vents. But tonight I wanted a bath even more than instant sleep and steered my aching body toward Free's back door.

When I inserted my key it turned easily, without the *thunk* of the lock's tumblers. I must have forgotten to lock it when I was in last, I thought, whenever that was. I pushed the door closed with my foot and stumbled to the bathroom.

My clothes were too muddy to add to the hamper, so I left them in a pile on the floor and brushed my teeth while waiting for the tub to fill. I'd spiked the water with gardenia oil to purge my nostrils of the mental scent of other people's dirty laundry, and I tried to wipe the scene I'd witnessed from my weary brain as well as I lowered my body into the steaming water.

"Steam it," my gymnastics coach had always advised

for any injury sustained in the course of vaulting over barriers, swinging under and over bars you had to be boosted to reach, and doing no-hand cartwheels on a beam only four inches wide. That and a few splints and surgeries had kept me going nine years in the sport. Until I sustained one that wasn't going to heal if I continued. I smiled, wondering what the docs would say about the evening I'd just spent.

My eyelids closed as soon as the rest of my body was submerged in the fragrant water, my neck coming to rest in the foam contraption Free had designed to keep one's head above water while the rest of one dozed.

I'm not sure how long I lay there, letting the weight of the world drain from my limbs. It must have been nearly an hour, because when the cooling water signaled my flesh to move, my watch on the edge of the tub read 1:18. I gave my hair a quick shampoo and hauled myself out.

My lids stayed mostly shut, hanging on to sleep, as I rubbed myself dry and pulled on one of Free's white T-shirts from the underwear shelf in the bathroom cupboard. On me it was the length of a nightshirt.

Already I was feeling one of Free's down pillows beneath my head as I padded toward the bedroom, reflecting that although I missed her like crazy, it was a real treat to have the use of Free's cozy cottage while she was gone.

Not even the closed bedroom door rang a warning bell in my besotted brain; Free'd probably closed it when she left.

My eyes opened wide, though, finally, when I pushed the door open to see that the bed I had been longing for was now definitely occupied. Beyond an empty wheelchair lay a man, his head propped on both of Free's pillows, his thick hair and beard making him look like the wolf in Granny's bedstead. It took my startled mind a moment to recognize him: Jake, Denny Lockett's big brother.

I said, "I don't remember inviting you."

"Denny told me you were quick," Jake said with a cocky smile.

"He told me nothing about you," I said. "Jake."

He frowned, the expression making him look more like the man I'd seen shouting in the Squatters' clearing.

"As your brother says, I'm quick," I couldn't resist saying. "Though at the moment I'm more in need of sleep than can-you-top-this."

It was true. Maybe I was too tired to see this man as a potential threat. Or too confident that the brothers were unaware of my presence when they had their shouting match at the camp. I believed his outrage when he thought his brother had killed Bercain without waiting for him. Of his brother's innocence I was not so sure.

"How did you get here? And why?"

"Why? My esteemed brother thought I was too conspicuous in town. People might start asking questions. Especially if they found out I was his brother. The police are keeping a pretty sharp eye on that camp.

"As for how, Denny thought we should have a little chat with you, see what you'd learned. So we came to your rig, but you weren't there. This, however"—he lifted a post-card from the night table—"was in your mailbox."

I made a weary gesture, so he read it to me. "*Paris is great. I needed this vacation. Next week Florence, then Venice, before going on to New Zealand. Don't look for me before February. Love, Free. P.S. Have you forgiven me yet?*"

He looked up. "It sounded like an empty house to us. And Denny said you'd be cool with it."

" 'Cool with it'!" I hated being taken for granted.

"Yeah. He said you knew none of the Squatters had killed the asshole."

"And how would I know that?" I said automatically, then held up a hand. "No. I don't want to hear it. Not tonight. Serve it to me with my tea in the morning. I'm sure you must know where the teapot is by now."

I turned. "I'll be in the loft. Don't even think about

waking me before six." I took another look at my watch. "Make that eight." And I turned and left the room, wondering whether I'd be so cavalier about the situation if the man were able to climb a ladder. It didn't keep me awake, though, not for a minute.

CHAPTER
20

It wasn't the smell of tea I woke to; it was coffee. And the grinding of wheels on Free's arduously stripped hardwood floors.

It took me a confused moment, then I remembered: I had a houseguest. An uninvited houseguest.

"Shit." I said it out loud. My sojourn in serenity was at an end.

Well, I'd make him go back where he came from, that's all. Let him take his chances with the police.

Then I caught myself. If the man hadn't shown up on my doorstep, I'd have had to hunt him down, find out what he knew, why he wanted Bercain dead, even if he hadn't done the deed. And who else—including his brother—he thought might have.

"Get it together, Piper," I muttered.

I took advantage of his being in the kitchen and scrambled down the ladder and into the bedroom closet to get something to cover my nightshirt until I could change in the camper.

I tried a brown-and-orange African caftan I'd always admired, but the sleeves reached beyond my fingertips and the hem dragged on the floor. I had to settle for a red canvas work shirt. Not too professional, but, then, neither was a nightshirt.

I was in the bathroom brushing my teeth again when it struck me. I'd left the bathroom door open last night. I turned and stared at the tub. Jake had to have heard the water running, have known I was in the tub. And I'd fallen asleep there for how long? Would he have come in to sneak a preview of the *femme* P.I.? Would the wheels have wakened me? Would *anything* short of a bomb have wakened me while that lovely sweet water stayed warm? Who leaves the womb until they have to?

Then I shrugged and rinsed out my mouth. Not all that much to see in any case.

When I came into the kitchen, Jake was pulled up to Free's white kitchen table, munching on a piece of toast. He had pushed aside the chair at that end to make room for his wheelchair.

"Great bread," he said congenially. "Homemade?"

"From the Spotted Owl," I said shortly. "Do feel free to help yourself."

He ignored the implication.

I was supposed to stay on the guy's good side, I reminded myself. At least until I could pump him for information. I went to the fridge. "You want half a grapefruit? Pink?" The white was too sour for me.

"Pink," he said. "My favorite."

I turned sharply to see if he was mocking me, but I couldn't tell. His thick black beard and mustache effectively hid the bottom half of his face. And his eyes were so dark, they seemed to hide rather than reveal expression.

I turned back and lifted a big one from the hydrator, carried it to the counter. All the knives, I noted, were still in their tall, slotted holder. I tipped it to me and pulled out a medium-size one, which sliced through the grapefruit easily. Free was the only person I'd ever known who always kept her knives sharpened. But, then, she was the only one I knew who seemed to do everything effortlessly, perfectly.

Enough to give a person an inferiority complex. Of course, when the subject comes up, she always says she couldn't do what I do, but I can fill in the blanks: She wouldn't take such idiotic risks.

I set the half grapefruit and a serrated spoon in front of the smiling interloper and seated myself at the other end of the table. "Okay," I said, raising my own spoon, "it's lay-it-all-out-on-the-table time. What is your link to Bercain?"

He raised his. "And I should tell you because . . ."

"Because—for starters—you are a breaker-and-enterer and I am a licensed officer of the law."

His mustache twitched. A smile? My grumpiness intensified. Did I have to prove myself to each and every person on this island in order to get taken seriously as an investigator? Denny must consider me a marshmallow to think he could just drop his brother on my doorstep.

I leaned over the table and fixed the man with my most formidable look. "I don't know what your brother has told you, but the facts are these: Edmond Bercain hired me to find out who was putting up WANTED posters all over town making various slanderous charges against him. I suspect that that bright idea was your brother's.

"Then the man is clubbed to death and his wife hires me to find out who did *that*. She also confirms that Little Brother was having an affair with her. Motive Number Two. Then you arrive and make a scene about who wanted to kill him the most."

Jake's eyes widened, showing more white.

Aha, I thought, they hadn't known I was there! "Molly knows all," I said, wagging my spoon at him. I love having the upper hand.

But I got more than I'd bargained for. The man shoved himself back from the table, the wheels of his chair rumbling against the terra-cotta tiles of the kitchen floor so loudly, I instinctively recoiled.

He twirled the wheelchair like an angry exhibitionist.

"*This* is what *I* charge 'Edmond Bercain' with. A.k.a. Eddie Burkowsky, formerly of Sacramento, California, where he hit a pedestrian with his big souped-up car and was so accountable for it that he left the scene, then the state."

He was leaning forward in the wheelchair, staring at me with so much heat, I found myself hoping he didn't confuse my being hired by his enemy with complicity in the man's crimes.

"How long ago was that?"

"Six years. Six *years* it has taken me to find him."

Jake propelled himself back to the table with a single thrust of his large hands. I had to fight the urge to jump as the chair slammed back against one of the table's legs and rebounded.

"The police were a joke," he said bitterly, staring at his plate. "Did next to nothing to find him. Even though I'd given them two of the numbers and one of the letters of his license plate and a damn good description of the car."

He ran his right hand over his beard several times. "I saw the thing coming, *way* over the speed limit. So I stayed back from his lane, even though I was in a *marked* pedestrian crossing and had the right-of-way."

His dark eyes blazed as he raised them to me. "But he had to have been blind drunk—or a stone-cold murderer—because he never even slowed. Came barreling down that street and, at the last minute, swerved right *at* me. I couldn't get out of the way fast enough."

Another wiping motion. "Doctors said I was lucky to be alive. But you know what?" He leaned across the table; I reflexively leaned back a fraction. "I don't *feel* lucky. I *feel* like exactly what I am, half a man, married to this damn chair for the rest of my life."

Then Jake seemed to collapse from within, his shoulders slumping, his chest caving as though drained of oxygen. I let several moments of silence go by before I said quietly, "So you traced him."

His eyes rose to meet mine again. "You bet. The cops said forget it. The shrink said get over it. But no way. I was going to find that bastard if it took me the rest of my life."

His hands gripped the arms of the chair and he raised his body off the seat, held it there stiff-armed for several moments. Then, as though it had nowhere to go, it dropped back into the seat.

"Took me a year just to find out the guy's name, then another to trace him to Seattle," Jake said tightly. "We thought we had him. Den went there to track him down."

He slapped the chair arm again. "He found him too. Found what he'd changed his name to. Even saw him once, coming out of a bank. Then—" His fingers snapped in the air. "Now you see him, now you don't. The kid let him slip through his fingers."

Jake stared down at his thin legs, side by side in the chair. "Den stayed there, said he was sure it was just a matter of time before the guy surfaced again. But the bastard seemed to have dropped off the face of the earth."

The man shook his head, like a horse does as it paws the ground. "Den gave up, enrolled at the university, went on with his life. But I couldn't do that. What else did I have, baking bread all day instead of fighting fires in the Sierras?" He shook it again. "I survived the worst Mother Nature had to offer, only to be brought down by a cowardly drunk."

There was a silence, then I was surprised to hear myself say, "At least you didn't let it make you bitter." Cold, Molly, cold.

But he looked up, and our eyes connected again; his mustache even curled a little. "Yeah, I spent a lot of years there. I couldn't let go of it. It seemed like, until I could confront him, I couldn't move on. I became obsessed with finding the man, got a state-of-the-art computer and downloaded every database I could get my hands on. You'd be surprised how far you can reach on the Internet."

Then he added, "But you must know that, being a professional investigator."

I gave a noncommittal nod. Fact is, I have only a vague idea of what's possible on the Internet. The Web. All those toys. Back at the precinct in Chicago, a desk jockey ran all the searches, while us boys and girls in blue stayed on the streets where we belonged. When I'd come to the island I had neither the money nor the inclination to outfit my office with the latest electronics. So I've mostly depended on my mentor in Olympia for that sort of thing. He's mostly retired and has the time and money for computer games.

"What finally did it," Jake was saying, "was an ad on the Internet: *Prince Island cottage industry looking for international location. Former Sacramento entrepreneur, Seattle businessman . . .*

"I just knew it. That was the man. *Bercain.*" He shook his head in disbelief. "I thought I'd checked out every variation of Burkowsky. With an *i* instead of a *y*; with an *e* instead of a *u*; but I never thought of *c*." He hit the side of his head so hard it must have hurt. "Never a *c*."

"Easy on yourself too."

"You want to hear this or not?" Jake shot back.

I nodded, made a zipper gesture over my mouth. As though that had ever worked.

"Not much more to tell, I guess. Den was bored with college, went to the island to look, and ended up getting involved and staying here. He kept hedging on his reports. Maybe this was the guy, maybe not. He was 'going underground to smoke him out.' " Jake's eyes rolled toward the ceiling. "That's Den: melodramatic to the end.

"But then I didn't hear—he didn't have a phone—so finally I just came myself. He'd been telling me not to, and once I was here I could see why. Sleeping with the enemy." His voice was hoarse, as though it had to wade through years of anger, the residue clogging his throat.

"So," I said, trying to stay on target. "If you'd found him, what were you planning to do?"

He looked surprised for a moment, as though he'd never considered the question. Then the dark eyes grew opaque again. "You mean *after* I broke both his arms and legs?" He shrugged. "Turn him over to the law, I guess, let them put *him* in one of their little boxes, see how *he* liked living a half-life."

"At the camp you seemed to assume Denny had killed him, and you said, 'He was *mine*.' Not an intention to kill him yourself?"

His eyebrows rose admiringly. "What, do you have the place bugged?" Then he shrugged again. "If I met up with him on a dark night with a weapon in my hand? Who knows?"

"He was killed on a dark night, with a 'blunt instrument' in someone's hand."

"Then somebody got there before me," he said grumpily. "And it wasn't Denny. He'd have told me. No reason not to."

"So if neither you nor your brother killed him, you have any idea who did?"

His frown was remote. "The wife hated him, apparently. I'm sure she took up with my brother only out of spite. He's still a kid."

"Has he always been as political as he seems to be now?"

"*Seems to be* is the operative phrase. His idea of political action is to make trouble for whoever he sees as the bad guy of the moment."

"And Bercain was his bad guy?"

"Yeah. Not only because of what he did to me, but the guy was beating his wife, Den's new sweetie."

The last word was pronounced with particular scorn, making me wonder if Jake still had "sweeties."

I backtracked. "So you traced Bercain to the island."

"Yeah. I wanted to come right away, but Denny kept saying I'd be too conspicuous, people would ask questions. And he was finding a lot of other shit the man was into, thought we could get him on more than a six-year-old hit-and-run."

"So Denny had already hooked up with Maia and the others?"

"The crook had an interest in all their properties. Apparently he had ties to a bank that would wait until just the right moment to foreclose, when they had nothing left to fight it with."

Iris's husband leaving. And Maia's. Wait till they're helpless and move in for the kill. *Edmond Bercain is not a nice man,* Maia had said with hate in her eyes that first day I'd had breakfast with them. Did they all have similar grudges, or only those who'd joined the Liberation Brigade, the rest just hangers-on?

And Dorothy. Did she know where Amber spent her evenings? Had Bercain been instrumental in creating that pathetic "Love's Throne" with the profits from their misery?

Did we, in fact, have our own little version of Christie's Orient Express, with everyone taking her or his turn at stabbing the villain?

I excused myself and went to dress for a visit to The Queen.

CHAPTER
21

I WAS HOPING the hostess at The Queen's Rest wouldn't remember me. I'd gone there some months before with a client looking for her sister, who might have worked as a waitress there. As usual I'd had to be a little pushy to get the information out of her. You hope you don't have to do that twice with the same person, having used up whatever goodwill she had. But the trouble with being four-nine and pushy is that the person you hope won't remember you . . . probably will.

I timed my visit for 10:00 A.M., which I knew to be their break time between breakfast and lunch. As I walked from the near-deserted parking lot toward the faux-regal gray stone face of the place, I rehearsed my story. A variation on the truth, I'd decided. The late Edmond Bercain had been my client. He'd been afraid for his life, and among the suspects was a platinum-blond woman who was blackmailing him. He'd met with her several times at this restaurant, but she'd never divulged her name or anything else about herself. He'd hired me to find out who she was. His widow wanted me to continue the investigation.

Lame, I know; I was still working on it as I entered the waiting room, its floor-to-ceiling windows draped with red velvet, a red carpet runner leading through the interior arch. The modern-brothel look. I wondered again about the rumors that, along with the upper floors of the hotel, the place had rooms in the depths of its interior that were let by the hour.

I passed through the arch to the scene I had expected: dimmed lights, an empty hostess station, and empty tables beyond.

I turned right, toward the bar, the direction from which she'd come before at this hour. But it was empty even of a bartender. I retraced my steps.

The red runner continued down the center aisle of the dining room and into another, darker one beyond. And beyond that?

No one had to invite me twice down that yellow-brick—or in this case red-plush—road. Looking about me once more, I began my stroll down it with stagy ease, as though I knew exactly where I was going and had every right to be going there.

The second dining room ended at a wall covered with the same red velvet drapery. I checked with a series of small knocks, but it did seem to be a solid wall.

There was a door at each corner. To the right, a gold-framed sign indicated that rest rooms and telephones could be found in the direction of its gilt arrow. I checked it out, and the sign proved to be correct.

I headed for the other door, my I-know-where-I'm-going footsteps barely breaking stride when I reached the other, also-gilded, sign: PRIVATE.

Here we go again, I thought. But really, how many PRIVATE signs must there be on this island? Hundreds? Thousands? After all, didn't everyone who moved here want to be the last to come—including me? Looking, in one way or another, for our own private space? Besides, this sign was missing the NO TRESPASSING component, however much implied.

In any case, I was becoming immune to the word and

turned the burnished knob, which, surprisingly, proved unlocked.

Beyond the door was another, smaller room, furnished with the same "distressed" faux antiques, the same red velvet drapings as the outer lobby. If this was, in fact, part of the fabled trysting spots, I thought, at least the decor was truth in advertising.

TRUTH IN ADVERTISING. TWISTED TIMES.

Could this be where my tipster really meant to send me? Or was the platinum blonde the link between the two?

In the room was a small ornate desk. Its drawer was locked, as I quickly established. The only other furniture was a plush maroon love seat, which looked as though it might even be a real antique.

In the back wall was a mahogany door, which proved to be unlocked as well. Apparently, I thought, the management didn't expect snoops at 10:00 A.M., when even the public dining rooms weren't in use. I turned the doorknob.

The opening I stepped through was the depth of two standard walls. Doubly insulated for sound, I supposed, so the noisy ones would not disturb those satisfying their ids only with food. (Gray always said that when I came to visit he was glad he didn't have close neighbors. I caught myself using the past tense and quickly switched my focus to the present.)

The hallway I was now standing in looked to be the length of the back wall of the dining room and was also covered by the ubiquitous red carpet runner. There were five doors along the left wall of the corridor, with five names in ornate gilt letters above them.

LOUIS XIV, the first door read. Its black lacquer knob was unmarred by a lock and twisted easily. Inside was a room that struck me as too imposing to foster real relaxed sex. Across from the door was a huge armoire, also black lacquer, with doors of some red wood inlaid with ornate designs rimmed in copper.

The bed took up the entire rest of the room, its dark four posts draped in gold. A tapestry on the wall at the head of the bed pictured five nymphs dancing around a figure I assumed from his huge bow and arrow must be Cupid. I noticed how . . . lush the figures of the nymphs were. How lovely it must have been to live then, I thought to myself, when beauty included some meat on your bones.

QUEEN ANNE was scrolled over the doorway to the next room, also locking only from the inside, which I did. Here the bed was a canopied four-poster, its thick white hangings drawn back with gold-colored woven cords. The room was dimly lit, but what light there was seemed to be coming from beneath the canopy, and I peeked under to see that the entire top was a magnifying mirror, lit by the sort of round globes that frame a vanity mirror, only lower wattage. I hadn't known the queen was such a reader, I thought, maybe needing the magnification in her old age.

Do people really like this stuff, though? I wondered. My face looked twice its size in the thing. I wondered how one could arrange oneself so that the features one wanted magnified would be, without also magnifying the parts of the body already too large.

At that moment a droning buzz began at the far end of the corridor: a vacuum cleaner. Time to retreat, I figured, and slipped back into the hall and returned the way I'd come.

Only this time when I opened the door to the mini-lobby, someone was seated behind its desk.

At first I didn't recognize the hostess I'd met before. Her hair was now in a boy cut and black instead of blond. But the eyebrows that rose in disapproval were familiar enough.

I gave a lame smile. "I guess this isn't the way to the rest rooms."

She didn't answer. Had no one ever made that mistake before? Someone who couldn't decipher arrows? Or was the word *private* more prohibitive to someone who didn't carry it as the first name of her profession?

"And what is it you're looking for now, Ms. Piper?" she said dryly.

"You remembered," I said. "I'm touched."

Clearly, she was not.

"As a matter of fact, I am looking for someone," I said in my best professional manner. I crossed the room and sat, unbidden, in a chair nearer the desk. Square-shaped, it had claws gripping balls at the ends of its legs. Predator furniture, I thought. How charming.

"Edmond Bercain, whose death you may have heard of, was my client," I continued, at a leisurely pace that must have been maddening for the woman. "He was in fear for his life. With good reason, apparently."

"What has that to do with your being here?" the woman said coldly. "In an area clearly marked private?"

I briefly considered sharing my thoughts on privacy with her but decided she was not in a philosophical frame of mind. Cut to the chase. The extracurricular activities of the place probably weren't illegal, if they were providing only beds, not partners, for their guests. But they probably didn't want it advertised either, which gave me a little leverage.

"Since Mr. Bercain's death, his widow has asked me to continue the investigation," I said smoothly. "And she has reason to believe that he met with someone here, at least once. We were hoping to speak with her."

The eyebrows rose again. "Surely you don't expect us to know every woman who comes here—to *dine*—with every man," she said, carefully closing the ledger that had lain open on the desk beneath her arms.

Too late; I had already seen it. A reservation book, apparently, with the names of the rooms down the left-hand column—LOUIS XIV, QUEEN ANNE, VICTORIA—and dates along the top.

"She's a platinum blonde," I said, ignoring her response. "Quite striking, actually. I would expect her to be noticeable."

The hostess's gaze left mine, her features moving ever so slightly, as though trying to decide on an expression. She knew the woman. She also knew that her silence was telling me that.

"Even if I did recognize such a woman as being a patron here," she said emphatically, "it is The Queen's policy *never* to divulge the identities of her guests. *Or* their associates."

"Associates" was a new name for that connection, I thought. And personifying The Queen? These people were really into their work. Still, her reaction seemed excessive if the woman were only a patron.

"A patron?" I said. "My information is that she's an employee. Such as yourself."

Kendall's description didn't fit the woman before me, even when she was a blonde, but the flush of color to her cheeks indicated that I'd come close.

I moved to reassurance mode. "I have no interest in making trouble for the woman, or for anyone here," I said. "I simply want to talk to her." I put special emphasis on the word *trouble*.

The hostility didn't leave the hostess's expression, was only spiked by a trace of fear. Her right hand batted at an imaginary fly buzzing about her head. "She doesn't even work here anymore," she said peevishly. "She left last fall. *Without* notice," she added. "Now I'm stuck with all this." Her hand described a vague arc of the room and those beyond.

"Her name?"

"Flora. Flora Nightingale."

I snorted in amusement, which only brought a look of puzzlement to her classic features. "Flora Nightingale? As in Florence Nightingale?"

Her expression didn't change.

"The nurse?"

Only annoyance. "Well, she wasn't a nurse," she said. "Though she did talk a lot about 'serving our clients' needs.' She had this job; I was out front. Now I've got both. Not that I get paid any more."

I decided she really didn't get it. No history in high school? Maybe Flora's parents hadn't had any either. Or enjoyed a nasty sense of humor.

"Do you know where she went? When she left?"

"No," she said, adding bluntly, "We weren't friendly."

A rivalry? "Do you know where she lives?"

"No. And even if I did, she moved. Her last check came back."

"Would the manager know her current address?"

"*He* asked *me*. And she sure hasn't shown her face around here to pick it up."

I decided that was all I was going to get, and I rose. "Well, thanks for your time," I said cheerfully, as though she had given it willingly. "Ms. . . ." But she didn't fill in the blank. Neither did she shake the hand I proffered, so I took my leave, through the door that separated The Queen's public from her private services.

By the time I reached my office it was just after eleven, and my answering machine was blinking in series of four.

It had been so long since Gray's last call that the sight of a blinking answering machine no longer gave me an anxiety attack. There is a certain comfort in silence.

I listened to the messages as I took off my best P.I.-style trench coat and hung it on the brass coat tree that is my sole antique. Nothing urgent about messages one through three.

It was the fourth that stopped me in my tracks. Gray's voice was so full of emotion, it sounded as though he were strangling. "Hey, sweetheart," it said. "I just wanted to say hello, see how you're doing. I miss you. I'm still struggling with this thing, but— Well, I miss you, that's all."

I listened to the message again, hoping there might be some hint of an explanation I'd missed. There wasn't. I only realized I was crying when the tears reached the hand clamped over my own mouth.

I collapsed into the client chair and gave way to the tears.

CHAPTER
22

I RECHANNELED MY EMOTIONAL ENERGY with a resolve to end the games everybody was playing in this case. I stripped off my nice-girl outfit and grabbed my shabbiest jeans from my office closet, the ones I use when I do my quarterly housecleaning.

The only shirt of any warmth I could find was a mice-nibbled red sweatshirt that had gotten lost in a carton that included granola bars left in a jacket pocket. But what the hell; I put it on anyway, along with the offending jacket, now foodless.

At the top of my agenda: get a little plain truth-telling out of the Squatters. I wanted to narrow my *Suspects* list in short order.

I'd intended to enter the longhouse by the front door for a change. But I heard voices when I got to the stoop and paused.

"I did that last week."

"That's because you missed the two weeks before."

"Come on, guys. We need more energy here, more participation. What happened to all that early dedication?"

"There wasn't any. Only yours, Lockett."

Wasn't this where I came in? I moved to the north-side window again. They were all in there, at the table, though lunch seemed to be over. It would be criminal, my professional conscience reminded me, not to take advantage of this opportunity.

I headed for the main area of tents.

The first I knew to be Leonard's, the source of the gunshots I'd heard on my second visit. There were a dozen model airplanes hanging by strings from the tent roof, secured with safety pins. They were the kind you make from a kit, which furnishes the balsam and patterns. Leonard had added his own touches by crayon-decorating the planes with what looked like national flags, some from countries I recognized, some not.

Ready for an international war? At least there was no sign of the gun, though the tent's roof and sides had been patched with scores of pieces of gray duct tape.

The tent next to it, out of which Frank had come running, was now double-zipped, the canvas and netting both, with canvas straps knotted over them. Is this what was supposed to prevent Leonard's getting the gun again?

The next tent was so much larger than the others, I took it for an office. There was a battered black metal three-drawer filing cabinet, which served as a base for a long board full of books, the other end resting on a dresser that had probably been found in some Dumpster.

To my right was a desk—as makeshift as the bookcase, formed of a sheet of plywood on two sawhorses—holding a manual typewriter and neat stacks of papers. Only an ivy-patterned green comforter on an air mattress at the back told me it must serve as a residence as well, and a familiar green tailored jacket on a metal clothes tree told me it was Dorothy's.

I approached the desk, the tent roof just clearing my head. This was one place where my height would be an advantage, I thought, while Dorothy's additional eight or nine inches probably kept her bent most of her tent-bound hours.

I glanced through the papers on the desk. Lists of supplies ordered and received, daily schedules of assigned chores. Beneath a stack of old *Grace Guardian*s lay a large manila pocket folder, its tab unmarked. I peered inside, then, with a quickening pulse, emptied the contents onto the desk.

Cut-up newsprint and several pages torn from magazines slid out, along with a pad of plain 8 1/2-by-11-inch white paper and a rubber-banded packet of white security-lined #10 envelopes. Peppering the pile were scraps of cutout copy, mostly just letters of various sizes and colors but words as well. I could see *important* and *Club* and *card*. The next note from my informant?

Then I heard voices and footsteps on dirt. I began to shove the materials back into the folder but stopped. This was confrontation day.

I stepped leisurely out of the tent. Dorothy was approaching with Denny, the two deep in conversation. Denny's head was turned, talking in bursts of speech and gestures. But Dorothy saw me, and her body came to full alert.

Eventually, Denny followed her line of sight and interrupted himself mid-speech, his expression reassembling itself to a salesman's smile tempered by caution.

"Our friendly neighborhood sleuth," Denny hailed me.

"Don't count on it," I said. Then, "What's new? Any recent visitors?"

I kept my eyes on Dorothy's face as I said it, trying to judge how much she might know of Denny's brother and their past, but the stiff expression on her plain features didn't change.

"Not really," Denny replied smoothly. "I understand your friend Freedom is out of the country. A shame to have that trendy little cabin of hers standing empty."

"Oh, I don't think you have to worry about that," I said through a tight jaw.

"Ah, but I do. I worry about all forms of waste."

I gave the man my iciest stare. I'd been thinking of him as a well-meaning adventurer at best, a facile opportunist at worst. Now I regarded him with more suspicion. Was he primarily an innocent in his relationship with Kendall Bercain, maybe even being used to spite her husband? Or was his role more calculated? He'd followed the man all the way from California. And he found him, seduced his wife. And killed him?

Dorothy appeared anxious to get rid of the golden boy at the moment. Her anxiety told me she knew I'd discovered her secret. The question remained: Was she only the messenger or part of the message?

"Did you want to see me?" she asked, her head making a slight, perhaps unconscious gesture toward the tent.

"In fact, yes," I said. "We haven't really had a chance to talk, have we?"

She looked less than eager, but resigned to the prospect.

"Well, I'll leave you girls to it," Denny said, a smug smile curving his generous lips. The odd thought occurred to me that Denny might well look exactly the same as he did now at the age of thirty, thirty-five, forty . . . that smooth brow and rosy cheeks, the bright blue eyes—the face of the all-American boy. How long could it retain that look of innocence?

Dorothy was holding open the flap to her tent. I preceded her into it, not having to see where her eyes would look first.

Her expression didn't change as she turned the metal desk chair around and motioned for me to sit in it, not even glancing at the desktop. She herself moved to the rear of the tent, lowering her angular body to the narrow bed, her bony knees in their shapeless khakis reaching nearly to her chin. What was her story, I wondered, to be in this position in middle age?

"How is your case progressing?" she asked, her voice

sounding strained. "Amber said you'd been here asking her questions."

It surprised me that Amber had shared that information with her mother. Me, I was tired of secrets. "You've been sending me messages," I said. "Why?"

She didn't bat an eye. "Just trying to help."

"So you know about the white house?"

"Some."

"Does 'some' include Amber's involvement?"

"Yes." Stoic.

"So you wanted me to intervene somehow? Why haven't you done that yourself?"

"How many teenagers have you known lately? Anything you go up against, that's what they'll be sure to do." She moved her arms up and hugged her waist.

"What else do you know about the business? Was Bercain involved in some way?"

"I don't know. It wouldn't surprise me."

That was it? That was the extent of my informant's information?

"Why have you been sending the notes? Why not just talk to me?"

"You might not have listened. Questioned my motives."

"I guess I do. Why tell me about Denny's affair with Kendall Bercain?"

"It seemed like something that might be relevant. It does provide a motive, doesn't it?"

"For whom? Kendall or Denny?"

"Oh, I'm sure Denny wouldn't go that far."

There was something about the way she said his name that seemed to speak worlds.

"You're Denny's right-hand mate here, aren't you?"

"Hardly a mate," she said in a harsh voice.

I studied her face. She'd probably never been pretty.

Not like her daughter. Now her "mate"ing days were over? What had Sam said about Denny? That he'd bedded just about every female in the camp. Was Dorothy the exception? Were we talking simple jealousy here? Not that jealousy was ever simple.

"So you suspect Kendall as the murderer."

Dorothy shrugged. "She had the most to gain."

"Do you know her?"

"Not really. She was here a couple of times." Dorothy's pale cheeks flushed slightly. A vote for the jealousy theory?

"Okay," I said, "tell me about the tips. *Truth in Advertising* was the first. Meaning . . ."

She shrugged. "Only that what it said on the WANTED poster was true."

"Who was the source of that information?"

"Denny and Maia, mostly."

"What about the taxes and domestic violence?"

"Maia had all the financial information. Denny said Bercain beat his wife, and Mrs. Bercain confirmed it."

"And you believed them."

Dorothy's sour face turned sourer. "I believed Maia. Denny was . . . already involved, so his judgment might have been influenced. But he didn't really need that charge to get people to go along with the Brigade idea."

"And Kendall?"

"I didn't have much use for her," she said coolly. "A slumming rich lady." A pause. "But I believed her about the abuse."

Dorothy's face had darkened. Personal experience? I didn't want to pry into that, but it would reinforce her own motive to kill Bercain, another abuser.

"And the *cowardly act from his past*?"

"Denny said to trust him on that."

"And you did."

She shrugged, avoiding eye contact.

I took another tack. "Do you have any idea what brought Denny to the island?"

"No. I don't think he's been here very long, though. He asks lots of questions."

"Like?"

"Where the power lies, that sort of thing."

"Would you say Denny is into power?"

She allowed herself a small smile. "I think you might say that."

"So you went along with the Brigade."

"Not the break-in. I thought the posters were enough to get the point across."

I was silent a few moments, watching her face. "The white house," I said finally. "What do you know about the hostess there, or whoever she is—the platinum blonde."

A small frown. "I've seen her. I followed Amber once, then watched all the next day. Apparently she lives there. The other women come only at night. Then the men. Not hard to figure out what's going on."

Another sleuth, but with the sense to stay topside. "Have you confronted Amber about it?"

"Like I said, confrontation doesn't work with her. I did once, but it only seemed to increase the number of nights she went there."

"She hasn't tried to hide her going?"

"Oh, I'm sure she wants me to know."

Dorothy's face sagged with sadness. "Whatever I do, she'll do the opposite. I'm sure she blames me for her father leaving. I can't seem to get through to her. About anything."

"You can't just put your foot down? Forbid her to leave the camp?"

"How? Lock her in her tent?" Dorothy's voice was hard with sarcasm. "She'd just take off for good."

I sighed. Did I really want to have children, when

babies grew up to be teenagers? "Are you confident that she's using protection?" I asked.

"She's on the pill. I considered it the lesser of the evils when I first found out she was . . . sexually active."

"That's not the protection I meant."

She looked alarmed. "Don't they . . . at those places . . ."

"I don't know," I said, then thought to add, "If it's any comfort, I looked through a few windows last night and saw nothing that would indicate Amber is actually having intercourse with anyone. She might just be a performer there. Still, she ought to be prepared for anything."

Dorothy sighed. "At this age they think they're immortal. They actually think they can control their lives."

"Tell me about it," I said, and stood. "Which tent is Denny's? I need to ask him a few questions as well."

"The next one." She pointed down the path.

Great, I thought. She probably can hear everything that goes on in there every night. An insidious form of torture if she cared. I wondered whether hankering after younger men was a standard part of the aging process for women, as it was for men. I didn't really want to know.

"Thanks for your time," I said, and handed her my card. "If you find out anything more, will you use the phone instead of the scissors?"

Denny was not in his tent, but I located him down the line, in Sam's tepee.

The flap was closed, but I smelled it well before I got there: the herbal, musty odor of marijuana.

They were lounging against a log, facing the burned-out remains of a fire at the tepee's center. The pot smoke seemed to have absorbed all the oxygen from the air; I was not tempted to go beyond the entrance.

"Hey, Molly Piper," Denny drawled, making only

a token effort to raise his head. His eyes remained at half-mast.

Great, I thought. A lot of information I was going to get in his condition.

"Could I speak to you, please?"

"Sure." He made an expansive gesture with the hand that held the roach. "Have a seat. Wanna puff?"

"No, thanks," I said to both. "I need to speak to you alone."

"He's got no secrets from me," Sam said amiably.

"Don't count on it," I snapped, then, "Sorry. But this needs to be private."

"Ooo," Sam crooned, insinuation drawing out the word. "Way to go, Denny."

Not in this lifetime, I thought.

Denny looked pleased, got slowly to his feet. "What can I say?" he addressed Sam over his shoulder. "They all want me."

I backed out, and Denny ducked his disheveled blond head to follow me. His blue windbreaker was hiked up on one side, revealing a black turtleneck beneath. He didn't bother to straighten it, falling into step beside me as I headed back toward the parking lot at a brisk pace.

"So. How do you like your new roommate?"

"I'd like him a lot better if he'd been invited," I shot back. "Why bring him to Free's? What made you think I wouldn't turn him in?"

"Why would you?" he said mildly, his breath reeking of marijuana. "He hasn't done anything."

"Then why doesn't he stay here?"

I cast a sidelong look at the guy, whose smile had become more guarded. I enjoyed his not knowing how much Jake might have told me.

"Well, you know, it's kind of rough out here for someone in a wheelchair," he said weakly.

I changed the subject. "Why'd you and Kendall break

up?" I heard myself use the adolescent term, as though they were dating teens.

Denny had stopped smiling and seemed to be struggling with the question, again uncertain of how much I knew of the affair. If this is your idea of fun, Piper, I thought, you need to get a life.

"She got a note," he said finally. "It said I wasn't coming to this . . . appointment we'd made."

I looked directly at him then, confusion and hurt lining his face. Maybe he really did care for the woman.

"I didn't send it, but she didn't believe me. We both thought we'd been stood up."

Dorothy's handiwork. Should I tell him? Maybe better to tell Kendall; if she really wanted the relationship, she could get back in touch. I frowned at my thoughts. These days I was a helluva choice to play Cupid.

Suddenly Denny said, "Jake really is a good guy. Kind of a hard-ass at times, but basically a good guy. He's had a tough break."

Again the sentiment seemed genuine. Maybe I'd judged the kid too harshly, I thought. Nonetheless, I said peevishly, "I don't run a hotel. Especially in a house that isn't mine."

"But you'll let him stay?" Denny asked, laying on the charm again. "Just for a little while?"

"Until . . ."

Denny seemed unable to fill in the blank. "Until I can get things resolved here," he said finally.

"What 'things'?"

Denny paused, then said, "I have a lot of responsibilities here. I persuaded these people to do this, take a stand. I can't just walk away now, before they achieve their goals."

"And what are *your* goals?"

"Get their land back, with lower payments. Or at least get some compensation so they can move on with their lives."

Denny's apparent earnestness was persuasive. I could see why the others had gone along with him. Maybe the goal was even genuine, in addition to his brother's agenda and the needs of his own ego.

"Did you kill Bercain?" I said suddenly, hoping for the element of surprise to reveal something in his expression.

He did look surprised at least. "No. Why would you think that?"

"You mean besides the fact that you were making it with the man's wife and blamed him for your brother's injuries?"

He nodded slightly, acknowledging my information. "He was no good to us dead," he said without having to think about it. "We were going to hit him up for damages."

"You and your brother."

"Yeah. Being a hit-and-run, Jake never got a dime." His face took on an unfamiliar scowl. "Our mother had to sell the house to pay the medical bills. It sent her to an early grave."

For the first time I saw the face of Denny's anger, nearly as hot as his brother's. But that meant more motive rather than less, didn't it?

"So." Denny shifted gears again. "It's okay for Jake to stay there for a while?"

I sighed. "Free's away till February. I guess he can stay till then if he behaves himself." Now I was talking of someone probably older than I was "behaving himself." This job was aging me fast. It and a few other things.

"Thanks," Denny said with apparent sincerity. "He really is a good guy."

"So you say."

Back with the "good guy" that afternoon, I stood on the counter unpacking groceries and putting them on the high shelves while he sat in his wheelchair and watched. I'm not much for planning ahead as far as food goes. I only have a two-burner hot plate and a small fridge in the camper. Another in my office. I mostly eat on the run when I'm out, crash when I'm in. But I wanted to stock Free's cottage well, so at least she wouldn't be losing supplies in the bargain—a bargain she hadn't made.

"You're going to make somebody a wonderful wife someday," Jake said mockingly, gazing at my stockinged feet on the counter.

I glared at him. Marriage was not my favorite topic these days.

"But you're probably too independent for that, aren't you?" he went on, his voice lazy and baiting. He actually wagged a finger at me. "Be careful. Toughness takes its toll."

"You should know, shouldn't you?" I shot back, and saw the missile hit its mark.

"I'd call that a draw," he said in a tight voice.

I shut my big mouth for once, smacked a bag of Krusteaz whole-wheat-and-honey pancake mix onto the shelf. Why had I gotten this? I never made pancakes. The only times I cooked were at Gray's. My eyes began to fill. Don't cry now, I begged myself, and squeezed the lids shut, sending a couple of tears spilling onto my cheeks.

I busied myself moving things around on the canned-goods shelf while I fought for control. Jake, thank God, was silent.

"I cook," he said finally. "Maybe I could earn my keep."

I was surprised, to say the least. But I avoided looking at him, not wanting to see if he wasn't sincere. I seemed to be feeling more emotional by the hour. Maybe I should just be by myself.

"There," I said, closing the cupboards. "That should hold you for a while. I have to go."

"You just got back," Jake said, with a touch of hurt in his voice.

"A P.I.'s work is never done," I said briskly. "And I'm getting sick of this case. I want to wrap it up."

"Does that mean you think you're close to a solution?"

"I'm always close to a solution," I said. Whatever that meant.

CHAPTER
23

JAKE INSISTED on making me lunch before I left, and proceeded to create soup from what I'd brought—beans and ham and onions. He refused my offers of help, said to just sit at the table and keep him company.

He asked me a lot of questions—about my childhood, my early commitment to gymnastics, my relationships. He told me he'd always known he'd be a firefighter, on the front lines like that.

At first I kept my answers brief, guarded. But he seemed genuinely interested, said he wanted to know what went into making a woman as "strong and independent" as I.

I didn't tell him that I'd never felt less strong and independent, let alone why. But I did find myself telling him about my rape back in Chicago, at twenty-one—something I hadn't even told my parents.

"I went from thinking I had the world by the tail to feeling utterly powerless," I said.

His dark eyes regarded me gravely. "But you came back," he said. "You got your power back. Even stronger, would be my guess."

"So have you," I said.

He shook his head, the dark look returning.

"You just may not know it yet," I said. "But if you

weren't strong again yourself, you wouldn't want anyone else to be."

Suddenly, I felt a great need to see Mikah Horn.

A cold rain had begun to fall, and the woods along Wolf Road were a mix of deciduous bare branches and the deep green of ferns and evergreens, lapping up the rain like fertilizer. As Wolf became Bay Road leading into Grace, there were jagged juniper hedges studded with sage, as bright as pink tulips. And in a gray urn cornering the walk to a church, lavender snow crocuses were just opening their faces. Life was coming back, although in truth it had been there all along, concurrent with the cycle of death.

The curbs along Parsley Street were nearly vacant of cars. In six months they would be bumper-to-bumper along it, and the sidewalks would be full of vacationers, ready to make the cash registers ring with enough greenbacks to carry the shopkeepers and the artists and the restaurateurs through another winter.

I left my little Civic in Captain Pyrus's safekeeping and descended to the beach, my first stop in search of Mikah. I had asked him once why he always seemed to be there every time I came. "My people have always lived by the sea," he'd said, looking wistfully out toward the Olympic Peninsula. "That's why the Makah considered the whale our friend and only hunted for food. Those were our ways when we were an independent people. Not like now," he added bitterly. The words of his father?

Mikah was there, standing in the rain at the edge of the water. Only this time his stance was more angular, more guarded than I'd seen, and when he turned at my approach I saw that his face was painted.

A straight white line extended from his hairline down his nose, crossing his mouth and chin to his neck. More vertical stripes lined his cheeks and throat, added white fangs to his mouth, then disappeared into his ragged black sweatshirt.

There was something very familiar about the configuration of white lines on his dark face. Then I saw it: the carving I thought of as The Warrior Face. That and something else: the mask his uncle Attlu had been painting in the photograph in Mikah's room. Except that its features were frozen in time, while these had begun to run in the winter rain.

"Hey!" I called, but he remained there, watching, wary.

I stopped my advance, only lifted my hand in salute, then moved to the rocks and sat in front of The Warrior Face.

After a while he joined me, silently, sat on what I'd come to think of as his rock.

We didn't speak for a long time. He sat like a statue.

"I'm going away," he said finally.

I turned to him, startled. "Where?"

"Shelton," he said, in a tone that expected an argument. "I'll wait there till they let my father out of prison."

I didn't mention that he was only fifteen and had virtually no means of livelihood, said only, "But what about your mother? And Emily? They rely on you."

His heavy brows lowered and came together. "If I'm gone, then she'll have to stay home with Emily."

Did he know what his mother did on her evenings away? I wondered.

"But school, Mikah. If you left here, you'd be leaving school. And I'm sure your father wouldn't approve of that, even if it was legal. Education is the only way you'll have a future as an adult."

He shrugged again, turned away to stare down the beach, to where a *rosa rugosa* hedge marked the beginning of the private property of the King's Castle, its striped yellow-and-white beach cabanas tied shut now from the winter wind.

"My people didn't get their wisdom from any school," Mikah said roughly.

"Long ago maybe," I said, "when they could live off the sea and the forest. But now I'm sure the Makah insist that their young people get as much education as they can. So they can make their way in the world while preserving their culture."

I was aware of the inherent flimsiness of my last sentence. I knew that most Native American youths who lived off the reservations or who left seldom went back, seldom kept to "the old ways." The cultures were too conflicting. I could only hope that Mikah could do both.

Neither of us spoke for a long time. Then I said, "Mikah, I've taken the liberty of asking your mother whether she'd let me take you to Shelton to visit your father, if she won't let you go alone."

He turned, interest animating his rigidly painted face.

"She hasn't said yes," I hurried to say, not wanting to get his hopes up. "But if she doesn't want you to go with me, what would you think if I went myself to visit him, to tell him how you feel and see if he can't work out something with your mother, so you could see him more often, or at least be in better touch with him."

Mikah regarded me with more distrust than I'd ever seen him display. I had to remind myself that the natural distrust teenagers have of adults is always compounded in a cross-racial/cultural situation. God knows I had to deal with plenty of it when my beat included the black projects in South Chicago. Not to mention my private mission into its Hispanic Little Village.

"Deal?" I said, extending my hand.

"I guess," Mikah said sulkily, not taking it.

"Do you want to talk to your mother about it or should I?"

"You." He was quick enough with that answer.

CHAPTER
24

EMILY WAS NOWHERE IN SIGHT as I approached the Horns' apartment complex from the alley off Sand Run Road. The sand in the dilapidated box was the shade and consistency of mud in the steady rain, and a crumpled aluminum garbage can lay on its wounded side against the wall. I clutched the warm sack of cinnamon rolls to my waist under my yellow rain slicker, bending over them protectively, hoping the bribe would get me in the door again.

It didn't have to. As I approached the door to B-12, it opened and a tousled Astrid Horn emerged backward, pulling the hood of a bright blue rain cape over her head with her left hand while her right tried to rattle a key into the knob on the door.

She didn't hear my approach, my booted footsteps masked by the tapping rain on the concrete walk, so I said her name just before I reached her.

It startled her anyway. Her head jerked toward me with the wild-eyed alarm of an animal caught in the headlights on a moonless night.

"Oh. You," she said without any pretense of politeness.

She straightened, seemed to consider for a moment, then said, "You doing anything for the next half hour? I gotta go get more of that children's Tylenol, get her fever down."

"Emily's still sick?" I said without thinking.

But she didn't seem to notice my knowing more than I ought to, waiting only for my nod before she rushed across the little patch of brown lawn to the parking lot. Before I went inside I saw that the rope across the passenger door of her car had not been replaced.

The interior of the apartment smelled of bacon and cigarette smoke. The double sink was piled with dishes, both sides, a frying pan ringed with white congealed grease on top.

The cry I heard from upstairs was more like a whimper, and I followed it quickly through the empty dining room, up the stairs, and turned to the right.

Straight ahead, through an open door, an unmade double bed was strewn with discarded clothing, a pair of spike heels forming an off-kilter swastika where they'd fallen on the dirty pink carpet.

Emily's room was to my right and barely larger than the oversize crib in which the two-year-old lay on her stomach, her back arched, a sharp curl of sound rising from her that made my skin prickle.

Her blond hair had wetted to a dull brown, bonded to her head as the limp cloth of a cotton nightgown was to her back and legs. I touched her cheek with the back of my hand and found it hot and moist.

The only thing I knew about small children and fever dated from my teenage years, when my cousin Morgan visited with her prewalking baby, Starr, who developed a fever in the night and was dipped into a bath of cool water in the kitchen sink. But wouldn't Astrid have known if that was an effective remedy for fever?

I leaned to turn the child onto her back, found I had to lower the side of the crib to reach her. Were most two-year-olds kept in cages like this?

Emily struggled against my touch, making her body almost impossible to lift. When I got her turned over, her head lifted off the mattress, fixing me with feverish bright eyes.

Then she seemed to recognize me, and her head fell back, her wail winding down to a murmur. "Bites," she said, the guttural sound seeming to come from deep in her throat.

Warning me that she was a wild animal capable of biting? Or maybe, it occurred to me, she was remembering our first meeting making the luminarias and was condensing "bright lights" to "bites." Judging from Mikah's translations, Emily spoke in shorthand, conveying whatever she had to in as few syllables as possible.

"Yes, the bright lights," I said back to her. "For the parade."

Her eyes narrowed slightly, as though with suspicion. You really had to prove yourself with this one, I thought. Although wariness seemed to be a family trait.

"Let's try to cool you off a little," I said to her, and left to find the bathroom.

It was just across the hall. Steam coated the mirror, and a towel thrown over the door of the shower stall was still wet. I glanced at my watch: 4:21. Had Astrid just gotten up?

There was no bathtub to set Emily in and the sink was too small, not to mention gritty, so I grabbed a washcloth that had once been yellow and a yellower hand towel from a bar over the toilet, wet them with cool water, and carried them back into the bedroom.

Emily's eyes were closed and didn't open as I folded the washcloth in thirds and laid it across her forehead, then patted her chest and arms and legs with the damp towel. Her breathing began to quiet, and I found myself humming a song my mother'd sung to me to put me to sleep. ". . . and for me some scarlet ribbons, scarlet ribbons for my hair. . . ."

Then the kitchen door banged open, jolting Emily awake, and I heard Astrid's footsteps on the stairs. She had the bottle out of the sack when she came through the bedroom door.

Emily's head rose off the mattress again, the washcloth falling from her forehead.

"Here. Drink this," her mother said, shoving a spoonful of the red liquid toward her mouth.

I wasn't surprised to see Emily's lips clamp shut.

"Dammit, you nasty child, this is for your own good!" Astrid shouted, and Emily's eyes blazed back in reply.

"Perhaps if you mixed it with juice?" I ventured. Anything to break the stalemate. "Does she still take a bottle? Maybe she'd be more willing to feed it to herself that way."

Astrid shook her head distractedly and left the room without answering. Then I heard her in the kitchen slamming cupboard doors.

Emily lay back down and closed her eyes, and I went to recool the cloths. By that time Astrid was back with a bottle half full of a liquid that looked like either urine or apple juice. I was hoping the latter.

Surprisingly, she handed the bottle to me. Aware of their war of wills and willing to accept a go-between?

Emily grabbed the bottle and began sucking the nipple as though her life depended on it. Soon, closing her eyes, she curled onto her side, and her breathing began to slow again. I unwadded the dirty blue thermal blanket at her feet and pulled it up around her neck. Then Astrid and I tiptoed from the room.

I retrieved the sack of cinnamon rolls from the counter where I'd dropped them and set two on squares of paper towel at the places Astrid and I had occupied the last time, taking my seat.

Astrid seemed to be operating under similar assumptions as she smelled a quarter-full pot of coffee, dumped it out, and began making fresh.

The silence was a good deal more companionable than it had been when I'd invited myself in before. If my presence wasn't wholeheartedly welcomed, at least it seemed to be accepted.

I waited until Astrid was seated and we'd taken a few swallows and bites before I said, "I'm a little worried about Mikah. He seems so . . . disconnected. I think he really misses his father. You know, at fifteen a boy really needs a man in his life," I added lamely.

Astrid didn't look at me, but her mouth set into a flat line, very like her daughter's.

I decided to skip the part about the war paint and went straight to the question. "I just ran into Mikah on the beach. He spoke again about wanting to visit his father. And I don't know whether you've come to a decision about my suggestion, but I have business in Olympia"—not untrue— "and wondered if it would be okay with you if I took him along. We could stop at Shelton on the way."

She was silent for a while, her once-beautiful face set in hard lines. Then she said—more to herself, it seemed, than to me, "I'm the one puts food on the table. I'm the one looks after them. But all they want is their fathers."

She took a bite of cinnamon roll, chewed it ferociously. "She's been givin' me that evil eye ever since her father stopped comin' around." She looked across the table at me, her tone belligerent. "Like that's my fault? He never cared about her, wanted me to get an abortion from the beginning." She made a harsh sound in her throat. "Maybe I should've."

She took a noisy gulp of her coffee. "And Mike—if he ever knew his father, he wouldn't be in such an all-fired hurry to see him. The man's worthless. Absolutely worthless."

"Maybe seeing him will help Mikah find out for himself," I said.

She gave me another appraising look. "What's in this for you? Why should you care?"

My throat swelled, but I shrugged, tried to match her

offhand style. "I just like the kid. And I'm sort of worried about him, that he might . . . go down the wrong path someday."

"Then he shouldn't be going to no prison, should he?"

From upstairs came a long, low wail.

Her fists clenched on the table. "Well, I need him here. I can't deal with that one all by myself."

Her tone had the air of finality. I realized it would be futile to argue, would make me persona non grata in the future. "Then would you object if I went to see Mr. Horn myself?" I said. "On Mikah's behalf?"

She gave me another of her why-should-you-care looks. Then she shrugged. "Do what you want."

CHAPTER
25

I WENT STRAIGHT TO THE CAMPER that evening, leaving Jake to his own devices. I turned on the camper's little propane heater, happy that I had so little space to heat, and did my ablutions with water heated on the hot plate. Then I dusted my body liberally with Night Musk talcum powder and put on my favorite long flannel nightgown, blue with white lace, and my plush Wedgwood-blue robe, and settled myself against my bed pillows to study my case notes.

I resolved to keep my thoughts of Gray and the Horn family at bay and focus on the case that paid for my bread and butter—even though no one seemed to miss the man whose murder I was trying to solve.

Not the criterion, I reminded myself, and lay the notes about me on the bed in an orderly fashion. "Orderly habits make an orderly mind," my second-grade teacher had told us ad nauseam, and made periodic inspections of the contents of our desks to get readings on our psyches.

I tuned the radio beside my double mattress to KPLU, Seattle's jazz station, and let it play low, in counterpoint to the rain. In point of fact I love the rainy western Washington winters. More gentle than the snow of my midwestern home-of-origin, though the winds could challenge Chicago's. But all the more cozy indoors, hibernating along with the bears whenever you can.

My virtue was short-lived, however. Somewhere between scrutiny of the third and fourth piles of notes, sleep snuck in and claimed me.

I woke early to find sunlight slanting through the window, striping my bed. Maybe, I thought for a confused moment, I had slept through winter and this was spring.

I padded to the camper door and looked out, half-expecting to see Free's garden in full bloom. But there was only sun gracing its empty rows, and the sound of water.

Water? I'd told Jake he could turn on Free's underground sprinkler system if needed while he was there, but the rain of the day before had done a thorough job of irrigation. I put on my mukluk slippers and went to investigate.

Following the sound, I headed toward the back corner of the house, where my outdoor shower had been rigged with hose and showerhead—and I stopped dead. Jake was standing naked under the stiff spray of water.

My first thought was, another fraud? Then I saw that "standing" was an illusion. Jake had apparently managed to hoist himself hand over hand up the pipe and was now supporting his weight by gripping the pipe's elbow above the showerhead with his left hand, while his right sudsed himself with the soap I'd hung there from a shoelace.

He had his head back and his eyes closed while he slowly rubbed the soap in a circular motion over his chest, down his abdomen and his loins, then slipping beneath a full erection.

His upper body was at least twice the size of his lower, and the water rolled off his shoulders like a mountain stream over boulders, then slid through the crevices of his diminished hips and thighs. Then he dropped the soap and held to the pipe with both hands, pivoting slowly under the water's spray. The morning sun seemed to flow with the rippling water, making his wet skin gleam.

I stood mesmerized until he saw me there, and all hell broke loose.

I'd never seen that much fury on one man's face. Even from thirty feet away Jake's dark eyes burned through me.

His right hand moved to cover his erection, his left still holding to the pipe, and he leaned to reach the wheelchair, on which his clothes were piled, just outside the shower's umbrella.

It was too far. One soapy hand had just touched the wheelchair's arm when his other slipped from the pipe, and Jake's dangling body dropped like a stone.

Instinctively, I rushed forward to help, but his head reared back and he yelled hoarsely, "Get away from me!"

I stopped, uncertain. Then his neck arched back again, those eyes burning, and he croaked, "Just stay away from me!"

Shaken, I beat a hasty retreat, and the camper door banged behind me.

My first impulse was to check my gun, kept under a pile of towels next to my mattress. It was loaded, the safety on. I stood holding it, telling myself that the anxiety I was feeling was beyond rational. Still, who knew what an anger that great could lead to? People had been killed for less in road-rage situations. Perhaps, I thought reluctantly, I should not eliminate Jake as a murder suspect.

I dressed quickly, in a jumper, tights, and turtleneck. I felt the need to be covered. I was glad I'd left my car nearby.

I opened the camper door cautiously but saw no sign of Jake. The sound of the shower was gone. The back door was closed.

My heart was beating so hard, it seemed to have affected my breathing. I thrust the gun into my bag, then took it out again. Was it really fear I was feeling? I hadn't needed a gun to handle most situations.

I put it back under the towels. Then I did what I always do when confusion threatens: I went back to work.

It was 6:05 A.M. when I reached the camp. Through the window I could see Iris and Maia doing food preparation in the kitchen. No sign of Dorothy or Denny.

Amber's and Dorothy's tents were still closed from the inside, as were Frank's and Leonard's. So far so good; I didn't want my presence known until I'd located Denny.

His tent, when I reached it, was secured from the outside with canvas ties. A note pinned to the flap read, *Out for the evening.* The note, on a strip of lined yellow paper, looked to have been used before, bearing numerous pairs of pinholes spaced a safety-pin length apart. Our lothario appeared to have spent many evenings—and nights?—out.

My disappointment at not finding him quickly changed to delight: I'd been given a written invitation to snoop.

I checked for observers, then made quick work of the ties and ducked inside, pulling the flap closed behind me.

Denny was not a tidy soul. He apparently did his laundry by drop-kicking each item into the nether regions of the A-shaped tent. Both sight and smell indicated that he had not visited a Laundromat in some time. It was also my guess that he and Kendall Bercain had not trysted in this tent. Unless the funky lifestyle had been part of the lure for her. Personally, I had found that living in a small space made good housekeeping a necessity. Not that I'd ever tell that to my mother; why ruin her image of me?

The bed consisted of a dirty mattress on a platform along the back, topped by a twisted red-plaid sleeping bag. A rough wooden crate served as a bedside table, holding a black-and-silver boom box that looked brand-new and a square standing flashlight at ground level. On top was a small white alarm clock, a legal pad of the same yellow paper as the note, and a Write Bros. ballpoint pen, medium-black. Several sheets of the pad were rolled back, the one visible reading:

STAGE TWO

Behind schedule. Aim for summer.

1. *Make more contact with the community. Clubs and jobs. Sports.*
2. *Jobs: gardeners, housecleaners, construction, handyman.*
3. *Clubs: Lions. League of Women Voters, Gardening, Friends of Library. Ultimately: Chamber of Commerce.*
4. *Churches: Frank and Leonard? Dorothy? Mainstream sects.*
5. *Sports: Pickup basketball games? Community baseball?*

In another crate to the side was a stack of what were labeled *position papers*. I picked up a few: *Position Paper #4: Vegetarians, Vegans, and Carnivores—Rights for All?*; *Position Paper #1: Equal Shares, Equal Duties*; *Position Paper #5: The Personal vs. The Political Path.* They were all single-spaced, several pages each, in what a quick skim revealed to be high-minded prose reminiscent of Philosophy 101, all apparently typed—inexpertly—on the same typewriter.

That typewriter appeared to be behind me, on a make-shift desk rigged of a sheet of plywood spanning two stacks of cartons. The machine was an old manual Royal, and there was an untidy stack of papers on its right, most of which seemed to be correspondence. I lifted the stack and thumbed through, finding some from local, more from mainland media—Emerald, Seattle, one Tacoma—requesting information and/or interviews. All were dated no more recently than last summer. Had the encampment's fifteen minutes of fame come and gone?

The only other object on the desk was a decapitated Diet Pepsi can, holding a collection of pencils, ballpoint pens, paper clips, stamps, and rubber bands.

The cartons the plywood desktop was laid on were set

upright, two on each side. The whole desk would have to be dismantled to see what, if anything, they contained, but I peered into the space between them that served as the knee-hole of the desk.

I could see little in the dim light of the closed tent, so I got down on all fours and crawled under, thought I saw something tucked into the far flap of the canvas where tent met ground, and crawled farther. It seemed to be a shoe box, and I pulled it toward me, backing up a little until there was enough light to make out the contents.

There were two packets of letters secured by rubber bands, both addressed to Denny Lockett at a post-office box in Grace. My curiosity rose another notch.

The first I lifted out comprised eight square envelopes of a blue linen weave, addressed in a graceful hand. In the upper left-hand corner the return address read *Kendall Merritt Bercain*, also at a post-office box rather than her home address.

The second packet interested me even more. There were maybe a dozen personal-size plain white envelopes, bearing the return address, in a bold square hand, of *Jake Lockett, c/o The Timber Room, Sonora, California.*

But the third object in the box was the real surprise. Also secured with a rubber band, there was a stack of plastic rectangles the size of ATM cards, pure white except for a gold engraving of a bird in the upper left-hand corner. A nightingale. I rubbed my thumb across the surface of the top card and felt a series of raised bumps—the open-sesame, I was sure, for a certain white gate in a certain white fence, to a certain white house, hiding in plain sight.

For a sleuth, such a find is as thrilling as gold bullion must have been to a pirate. But the thrill was short-lived, as I heard voices approaching the tent. One was Denny's; the other, Sam's.

Hurriedly, I put all three packets back in their box and returned it to its hiding place, only at the last minute pulling the top envelope of Jake's packet from its band and slipping it into the pocket of my windbreaker.

Sam's voice was saying, with a querulous edge to its bass, "Then who's going to do the work around here? Do you have any idea what it takes to keep this place running? While you're off hobnobbing with the upper crust?"

"Damn!" Denny muttered, from right outside the tent now. "I closed this thing up before I left. Damn that kid! Frank's gotta keep a closer eye on him."

Then he threw the tent flap back and they were coming in.

"See anything missing?" Sam said.

Denny crossed the tent and reached under the mattress, pulled out a plastic bag in which I saw a flash of green as he raised it. "Mmm," he grumbled. "Seems to be all here."

I smiled at his priorities.

He sat on the bed, brown tweed trouser cuffs showing over shiny black shoes, and reached into the lower compartment of the crate, pulling out a packet of cigarette papers. "Want one?" he said.

"Sure," Sam replied from beyond my sight, and I saw Denny's fingers roll two reefers, heard the click of the lighter, and smelled the unmistakable odor of marijuana.

I huddled beneath the desk, barely breathing, as the two smoked in companionable silence. I could see the bottom of a sports coat with suede pockets draped over Denny's tweed-trousered legs, bent almost double as he sat on the sleeping bag on its low platform. His two worlds at once, I thought, wondering whether it was Kendall or Ms. Nightingale picking out his new wardrobe now.

"You wanna come confront Frank about Leonard?" Sam said, in a lazy voice that threatened little confrontation.

Denny's answer was to stretch out on the bed, his left arm over his eyes. I shrank back beneath the desk, squinting in an (only slightly) adult version of the child's conviction that if she can't see you, you can't see her. Even if he turned toward the desk, I doubted he was low enough to see me, but I hoped not to put it to the test. On my last case I'd spent a miserable half hour under someone's bed, just missing being crushed. Still, I had found critical information in the process.

"If you're gonna sleep, you might want to take off those fancy duds," Sam said sourly. "What the hell are you got up for like that, anyway, this time of day?"

"A business meeting," Denny muttered. "Just another business meeting."

"Seems like you've been having a lot of those lately. What the hell're you into, Lockett? Seems like you're getting farther and farther away from the original idea of this thing. Remember? The rich squeezing out the poor? Power to the people?"

"Mmm," Denny mumbled, sounding half asleep. Then I heard the long intake of breath signaling another drag on the reefer.

"Okay," Sam said, sounding discouraged. "I'll see ya later."

Denny didn't answer. There were two more drags on the joint after Sam left, spaced widely apart, then silence. I found myself worrying about whether the reefer's fire had been put out.

I'd been sitting cross-legged beneath the desk, now leaned forward over my feet in a yoga position that would have made T-om proud. Denny's breathing had become almost silent, and his position had not moved for the past ten minutes. I couldn't see his right hand.

I waited as much longer as my limited patience could stand, then eased myself forward, nudging the folding metal desk chair farther to one side so my knees and elbows wouldn't knock it accidentally as I cleared the desktop and stood.

Then I began backing out of the tent slowly, my gaze fastened on Denny, alert to any movement.

I was halfway out when he stirred and his head swung toward me, the eyes open if not fully focused.

Quickly, I reversed my direction and took a step toward him. "Oh," I said, "I'm sorry. I'm interrupting your sleep. I'll come back later."

But Denny sat up, swung his shiny shoes over the edge of the platform. "No need," he said. "I was only resting my eyes. What can I do for you?"

He'd said it with the automatic good cheer of a born pitchman. It struck me how different the brothers seemed to be from each other, and I wondered how much the accident might have had to do with those differences. Fruitless wonderings, of course.

Focus, Piper.

"I . . . I have some questions about Jake's injuries. But they can wait."

"It's okay. I'm awake. Sort of. This is something you can't ask him?"

"Well, I guess I thought I'd get your take. On his legs, whether they've had all the physical therapy that . . . might be useful. Maybe I could encourage him to do that."

Denny laughed, a full belly laugh. "I guess you don't know my brother. He'd drag himself up Mount Everest if anybody'd let him. The spine was fully severed; he's had to make up for it by strengthening his upper body."

Then he smiled at me, a bit slyly. "Taking an interest, huh? That old dog."

I felt my eyes widen with shock. "Of course not," I snapped. "I just—" I frowned. "Go back to sleep." And I made a hasty exit. Frontward.

CHAPTER
26

I WAITED UNTIL I reached the office to read the letter in my pocket.

There was no message on the machine.

I dropped into my swivel chair and took several deep breaths. With all the running I did, you'd think my lungs at least would be in good shape. But nothing felt in great shape these days.

I opened it. The handwriting on this letter had an angry slant to it. It was postmarked December 26, from Sonora, California. No greeting inside, just the direct launch of an attack.

> *What the hell is happening there? I haven't had a letter from you in two weeks, and you don't even have a damn phone. Do you even remember what you're supposed to be there for? Here I am stuck in wall-to-wall snow while you're off playing King of the Hill. Or the woods or wherever you are. Probably the whole town by now. You always have to be king, don't you?*
>
> *So is it him or not? How big can that island be?*
>
> *Write me! Now! Better yet, call. If I don't hear from you by New Year's, I'm coming myself, if I have to wheel the damn chair all the way there.*
>
> J.

By "New Year's." As in New Year's Eve? Damn. From what I'd seen of the man, he could easily handle the physical part of braining Mr. B.—with or without a blunt instrument.

I tried calling airlines to see who might have carried one Jake Lockett to Seattle on the thirty-first or the first, then shuttled him to Prince Island. No one would say. Not even to "Mrs. Lockett," who did a fine job of sobbing in her anxiety.

Same no-story from the Orson Naval Base field, though at least they told me that if he wasn't military, it was highly unlikely they'd delivered him to the island.

I broke the connection and stared at the receiver in my hand. I'd been hoping Gray would have called again. Clearly, he'd done it when he knew I wouldn't be there so he could just leave a message, but at least it was better than nothing.

Then I realized: I could do that too.

It was after 8:00 A.M., and he always left the house by 7:30. I punched in the numbers, my heart beating in my ears.

I didn't know whether to be relieved or disappointed when, after the third ring, the machine answered.

"It's me," I said in a bare whisper. "Thank you for your message. I miss you too. I just hope . . . well, that you're taking care of yourself too. Call me. If you want to."

Stupid! I castigated myself as I hung up the phone. What a stupid thing to say!

I fought back tears and dialed Simon's number in Olympia. It was time for me to let him run my list of suspects through his computer bases, see what nasty secrets might lie in their pasts.

I nearly broke down and cried at the sound of his voice. Simon is my rock. He really listens, and he doesn't judge. I know I can tell him anything and he'll never slip out from under me. My rock. But I wasn't ready to talk to him about Gray yet. Not on the phone.

"I'm heading across to the peninsula tomorrow morning," I said after I'd given him my list—my *complete* list, including both Lockett brothers.

"I'm going down to the penitentiary in Shelton. And I could go on to Olympia if you're going to be there and would like some company."

"If the company is you, always," Simon replied with his usual gallantry. "Who's in Shelton?"

"Not case-related," I said. "It's the father of a boy I've gotten to know here. His mother won't let him visit the prison, so I'm going as sort of a surrogate. Also, I can use a change of scene. It's become a real pressure cooker here and I need to clear my head. You're always a help to me with that."

"Glad to be of service," Simon said. "Shall we expect you for dinner, then, tomorrow evening?"

"Sounds wonderful," I said, feeling better already. Ursula, Simon's cook/housekeeper, has a voice that could shatter glass, but her cooking's to die for, and Simon's brain is both clear and calming, blowing away the chaff to leave the grains of truth in sharp relief.

Then I went to see what I could find out from Thaddeus Belgium. Maybe I could trade him my hard-won knowledge of "Love's Throne" for any hard evidence he might have uncovered on the murder.

Chief Belgium was in his glass office in the corner, with more of the island brass than I'd seen since my last major case: Frank Lautenberg, the Port Angel chief of police; Claude Forbush, Sweetbay's chief; Jackson Kellermyer, Island County sheriff; and Captain Truman Newell from the Orson Naval Base. Any relation to my case? I wondered. Did they see Bercain as that important?

They looked far from winding down, so I detoured to my friend Ellie's desk and sat on a neighboring chair until she was through with the call she was on.

While I was waiting, I looked around. Officers Gersch and Burrows were not at their desks. Karen Pasco was tapping at her computer keyboard and either hadn't noticed me or was pretending she hadn't.

Karen and I had never taken a liking to each other. She'd been the only woman in the law-and-order system when I arrived on the island more than a year ago and had apparently preferred it that way. Skilled and striking both, she liked being the center of attention.

I probably should have been flattered that she considered me any competition for the position. Not since my acting days in college had I played Belle of the Ball. In fact, in my line of work it's wise to be inconspicuous. Gone are the days of gypsy skirts, all-up-the-ear earrings, and all-up-the-arm bracelets. Ms. Molly now lies low.

"So," Ellie said when she finished her call, turning her sharp green eyes on me, "what's going on?"

Ellie Foster is a good listener, but sometimes too good. You find yourself spilling your guts, and it ends up being more guts than you wanted to spill. I looked at her guardedly.

"That much?" Ellie said dryly. "You and Gray still holding each other at arm's length?"

"So it would seem," I said wearily.

"You still don't think you should break the impasse?"

"I don't know. This can't go on forever; I'm a wreck."

She seemed to be waiting for me to go on. So I started filling her in on recent events, including my uninvited neighbor.

Pretty soon the sharp eyes sharpened further, and I found myself weighing every word. Finally, she could hold it no longer, held up a stop-right-there palm.

"Let me get this straight," she said. "You overhear this guy going ballistic because somebody killed the man he wanted to kill. If—" She raised a finger just as I was about to point out that that was evidence of his innocence.

"If," she repeated, "the whole scene wasn't staged for your benefit.

"Then," she went on, "the guy breaks into Free's house, climbs into Free's bed, and *you* say fine, I'll just go sleep in the loft!"

I was glad I hadn't mentioned the possibility of his having peeked in on me in the tub. Instead, I said, "The man can't climb. I was perfectly safe."

"If the wheelchair also is for real. How do you know he's not one of your insurance fakers pretending he can't walk?"

I really hadn't wanted to tell her about the incident at the shower, but I guessed I was going to have to. I got to the part about his exploding when he saw me watching, when Ellie had a little explosion of her own.

"That's two temper tantrums in two days," she said. "Not a good average."

"I know," I said, "but I shouldn't have stood there watching. Naturally he was embarrassed that I'd seen him, especially since—" But I'd left that part out.

"Since?" Ellie pressed.

"Since he had an erection," I mumbled.

For a moment Ellie's face went mercifully blank. Then she began, "But then he's not really—"

"I guess that's not affected," I said. "I heard that about Christopher Reeve's injury. They plan to have more children."

"Well," Ellie said. "I guess that makes him doubly dangerous."

" 'Doubly'?"

"As a potential killer and a man trying to get into your pants."

"Oh, really!" I said. Ellie's bluntness was nothing new. It was generally attributed to the nature of her job—and the fact that she came from New York.

"I'm sure he has more serious things on his mind," I said forcefully.

Ellie's green eyes studied me a moment. Mine looked away first.

"You're attracted to him," she declared, as though it was a simple statement of fact.

"Don't be ridiculous," I snapped.

When I looked up she was still giving me that look.

"May I remind you," I said, "that I already have a man?"

"Not lately," Ellie said.

That really pissed me off. "You're saying that a few weeks without sex and I'm lusting after every man I see?"

"Not every man," she said coolly. "This man."

I opened my mouth, but nothing came out. I looked again at the chief's glass office, but he and the others were still going strong. "Look, I can't wait," I said, standing. "I've got work to do." And I started moving off.

"You ought to take something for that overactive imagination!" I threw as a parting shot.

I spent the rest of the afternoon checking out the rest of my suspects' alibis. Every one checked out. Even Franklin Watts, who turned out to be a scion of carpet cleaning. Finally, the phone hadn't rung and I could find nothing else productive to do, so I headed for home.

CHAPTER
27

I WAS HOPING not to encounter Jake before my leave-taking in the morning, but that was not to be.

From Wolf Road I saw the flute of smoke rising from Free's chimney. Then as I turned into the drive I could see a strip of Jake's dark face framed by the raw-silk drapes at the front window, his wheelchair making a faint box outline below.

Unconsciously, my foot hit the accelerator, making a *scrunch* of gravel, then another as I braked to a stop at my camper steps.

I jumped out and up the steps way faster than I needed to.

What is my problem? I asked myself. I'd faced down whole gangs in South Chicago, innumerable handguns in nervous hands, and a serial killer in my own backyard. But one angry guy in a wheelchair was getting me rattled? Get it together, Piper!

The camper was *cold*, felt colder than the air outside. I huddled my windbreaker around me and began searching the cupboards for soup. I'd planned to eat out but decided all I really felt like eating was soup; I could fix that myself. I just felt tired—tired of the case, tired of my impasse with Gray, pretty much tired of my life.

Buck up, Piper, I told myself, now it's you playing the self-pity violin.

I stiffened as I heard the crunch of narrow wheels on the gravel drive. I stopped with the plug to my hot plate halfway to the outlet. Then I had one of those full-body shivers that start at the shoulders and move down, making you shake like a frail tree in an island wind.

There was a rattling sound against the side of the camper. Thrown gravel?

I went to the door, waited. Maybe he'd go away.

More gravel, then a call. "Come out, come out, wherever you are."

Reluctantly, I opened the camper door. Jake was sitting in his wheelchair in the drive, about halfway between cottage and camper. "Truce?" he called. And when I didn't answer: "I've made dinner. I even had Denny bring the ingredients, so no cost to your friend."

I considered saying I'd already eaten, though in fact I hadn't had a thing all day. Not like me. Not like me at all.

I looked down at my denim jumper. "Do I have to dress?"

"I did," Jake responded, gesturing to his fully clothed self. Even at the distance his smile made his teeth shine white between beard and mustache. A changeable fellow, this. A danger sign?

"Doubly dangerous" were Ellie's words.

Nonsense, I said to myself. What was I, a slave to my id?

"No business talk," Jake said as he seated me at the table next to the fireplace in the living room. To my left, a healthy fire was already burning, the red-orange flames licking the bare wood, turning it rosy with heat.

Alarms were going off in my head like crazy, but the fire was so warm, and my camper so cold, and there was this heavenly fragrance of seafood and saffron coming from the kitchen I'd just been hustled through. "I can't promise," I said in a voice I wished sounded stronger.

But Jake was already rolling back to the kitchen.

Free's transported kitchen table was covered with the handmade patchwork cloth and napkins she brings out for special occasions. It didn't surprise me that Jake had managed to haul the table and the wood for the fire into the living room. Though maybe Denny had helped. A distraction project for the nosy P.I.? If I hadn't felt weak from hunger and my muscles rubbery from the heat, I'd have left right then. I think.

On the table, a fat crimson candle burned in a copper saucer I didn't recognize, but which looked like an ashtray. That's when I realized the other faint odor I'd detected: marijuana. Is that what Jake had used to lull his anger and bolster his courage? I hadn't smoked pot since my first experimental college days and hoped I'd refuse if it was offered. Though I could have used some lulling.

Jake wheeled out of the kitchen then, bearing Free's big iron skillet on a wicker tray in his lap, a patchwork oven mitt on each hand. None of Free's belongings looked harmed, but I wondered what she would have said about the use to which they were being put. Probably less about the use than my participation in it. I could hear her "What were you *thinking*?" echoing in these very rafters.

All such thoughts were stilled, however, by the tastes of mussels and clams and rich hot sausage that spiced the saffron rice filling my mouth. "This is *delicious*," I said before I'd even swallowed.

Jake beamed, producing a bottle of red wine and two glasses from the side pack strapped to his chair. He poured for us both before he tasted his own plateful. (I'd jumped the gun again.)

"Where did you learn to cook like this?" I said between my second and third mouthfuls.

"It's how I make a living," Jake said. "I fixed this paella

for The Timber Room in Sonora and they adapted their kitchen just to accommodate me."

"I can see why," I said, plucking a mussel from its shell with my tongue. This was good: Food and weather were safe subjects.

But a few moments of serious eating later, Jake said, "I'm sorry I blew up this morning."

I looked up warily. This was a less safe subject.

"I just never seem to get over what's happened to my body."

I said nothing, chewed with lowered eyes. What was I going to say: Your torso alone beats most men's entire bodies? Not to mention the handsome head.

"The bastard's death does give a little closure," Jake pressed on. "But I didn't kill him. And neither did Denny."

"I thought we weren't talking business," I said, noting how the reflection of the fire lit his dark brown eyes.

"I just wanted you to know," Jake muttered, returning his gaze to his own plate.

We ate in silence for some time. A companionable silence I would have said, except for the sexual tension that crackled like the fire heating my left side to the point of acute discomfort.

It's what finally got me up. It had become obvious that neither of us could eat another bite, although several still remained on our plates. I stood and picked up both plates, held them over the rest of the paella in the iron skillet. "How do you feel about recycling?" I asked.

"Go for it," Jake said. "But"—he reached out and caught my hand mid-dump—"only if you promise to finish it with me tomorrow."

I dumped them anyway but shook my head. "I'm off first thing in the morning and will be staying with my mentor in Olympia tomorrow night."

"A mentor," he said, bringing his fingertips to his lips. "I can't quite picture that."

"What?"

"You having a mentor. You don't seem the type to follow anybody."

I had to laugh. "The Chicago Police Department would agree with you. I caught a bullet being somewhere I wasn't supposed to be, doing something I wasn't supposed to do. By myself."

"You got fired?"

"More polite than that, but it amounted to the same thing."

"So you became a P.I."

"Eventually."

"I bet you're good at it."

"You sure couldn't tell by the progress I'm making on this case." I gathered the plates in one hand and the wineglass stems between the fingers of the other and headed for the kitchen. "I'm doing the dishes," I called back, "and then I'm off to get my beauty sleep."

You know that trick when somebody comes up behind you and bends his knees into the backs of yours so you cave? Well, let it be known that that works just as well from a wheelchair. Except that you've got a lap behind you to cave into.

I was sitting there before I knew what had happened, and he was turning my chin and kissing me before I could stop him.

Worse, I didn't want to. Everything about him was hard—his mouth, his arms, the shoulders my hands began gripping. They made me feel surrounded, safe, freed from the free will that had lately become such a burden. My head swam behind my closed eyes and I thought—hoped—I would pass out.

Unfortunately, I didn't. Hours later, when our passion had finally spent itself, I knew full well what had happened and my participation in it. *Avid* participation.

Jake was lying on his back on the futon pad we'd dragged to the fire, his eyes staring upward, a thin film of sweat making his skin glisten. Without turning toward me he said, "This is where you say I have to go and slip quietly off."

The hell of it was, I wanted to do just that. I wanted to be alone with my confusion and try to make sense of all the conflicting emotions I was feeling.

On the other hand, I wouldn't have put up much of a fight if he wanted to go another round.

"I guess you know what a terrific lover you are," I said sincerely.

His mouth couldn't resist a smile and closed in on mine.

"However," I said when I came up for air, "I do in fact have to go. I have a whole lot of thinking to do."

His eyes distanced again.

"I'm . . . involved. Have been for the past five years. And I love the man. It's just that things are sort of confused right now."

His profile had resumed its former stiffness.

"Dammit!" I said. "Don't make this about your . . . anything. I know I shouldn't have let this happen. I tried. Really."

Jake's gaze flicked toward me, a smile curling the mustache.

"Yeah, yeah," I said. "You're irresistible, we all know that." I flipped the back of my hand at his beard. He caught it.

"Really," I said. "I should have just said no. Now . . . I don't know what to do."

"Do I get a vote?" Jake said jauntily.

"I think you just did. Now I've got to come to my own decisions."

I had managed to disentangle myself and stand, holding my shoes and assorted garments. I didn't know what more to say, so I simply bent and brushed my lips across Jake's cheek above the beard and let myself out the back door.

I didn't think I'd sleep much that night, but I'd barely climbed between the sheets when I dropped into a deep and dreamless sleep, from which I woke only with the greatest reluctance the next morning.

CHAPTER
28

THE FERRY FROM SWEETBAY curves southwest to Port Juniper at the northeastern tip of the Olympic Peninsula, a half-hour ride. From there it's seventy-four miles south to the Shelton penitentiary, the launching pad for the Washington State Department of Corrections. All prisoners sentenced to a Washington prison go first to Shelton for intake rites.

From Seattle the route dips down I-5 to Olympia, around Puget Sound, and up Highway 101 to just above the town of Shelton—all pretty much a high-speed chase on the interstate. From Port Juniper, though, the trip is a mellow drive down the two-lane winding road of Highway 101, much of it along the deep blue Hood River, sparkling under the winter sun, and through the eastern portion of the Olympic National Forest, home of some of the largest still-virgin evergreens in the country.

I took it all in like a balm on my frazzled nerves, cracked my window to let in the glorious scent of wet forest. I never tired of it: It put me to sleep at night and woke me in the morning. Now I drove in a state somewhere between the two, relaxed but reasonably alert. The thought occurred to me, but was quickly dismissed, that my relaxation could be partly due to the release of sexual tension. But surely, I assured myself, I was above being ruled by my hormones. Wasn't I?

The thought brought a wash of guilt over me. How could I get sexual pleasure from anyone but the man I loved? But no sooner had I convinced myself that what had happened with Jake was a one-time aberration than the mental image of his face during orgasm sent a sexual jolt right through me.

Easy, girl, I told myself. Focus on the road ahead, not behind. You'll have plenty of time to obsess on the trip back.

The penitentiary, when I reached it, did not have the high gray walls of prisons I'd seen pictured. It looked not much different, actually, from an auto-parts manufacturing plant near my childhood home in Indiana—a one-story, windowless, concrete-brick structure trimmed in turquoise.

I stopped at an intercom along the driveway in and identified myself, recited the number of my private-investigator license, and said I was there to see a prisoner.

I felt more than gauche when I was asked if I was on the prisoner's visitor list and had to answer no. I had called the prison to ask the visiting hours, was told they were between 10 A.M. and 8:30 P.M. Fridays through Mondays. I didn't think to ask if I needed the permission of someone.

"I am representing the inmate's son," I said into the intercom. "He asked me to come since he could not."

"I'm sorry, miss," said the disembodied voice, "only visitors on the list can visit an inmate."

"Can I get on the list?" I asked. "Could I come in and speak to someone about getting on the list?"

There was a pause full of static, then the voice said I could park in the lot on the left and come through the front door.

I did so and found myself facing a man and woman behind a glass partition, like that of any hospital or doctor's office in the country—except for the uniforms.

I explained again who I was, showed my license, and said I wished to see Derrick Horn.

The woman, an attractive middle-aged blonde, explained to me—with more patience than I deserved—that the only people permitted to visit an inmate had to be on a list generated by the inmate himself. Those people were then given a background check and, if they passed, were notified—as was the prisoner—that they were permitted to visit him.

I tried to excise the frustration from my voice and asked if she could just look on her computer, please, and see whether the inmate's son, Mikah, was on such a list, thinking if he was, I could perhaps plead an exception from some authority on the basis of being Mikah's surrogate.

It was probably lucky that the time was only 10:20 A.M., the beginning of her day, and not later when she'd had to deal with scores of visitors, some perhaps as ignorant as I. She just sighed and began tapping the computer keyboard.

She went from screen to screen, pausing and frowning at each one, then finally turned a puzzled face to me, saying she could find no such inmate at this prison.

Nonplussed, I asked the obligatory question: "Are you sure?"

She said she was.

Had he come and gone? After all, how long a sentence could you get for assault and battery, even adding in the cultural bias? "Has he been here, perhaps, but was released?" I asked her.

"When was he brought to Shelton?"

I told her I didn't know. "His son's fifteen," I said, as though that was a measure. It was the only one I had.

The woman did more tapping and frowning. Then her blond eyebrows rose and she said that indeed there had been a Derrick Horn in Shelton, convicted of assault and battery. But that had been just over fifteen years ago. And he was there only five months before he'd been sent back to Seattle to face other charges. He had not been returned.

Other charges. I asked if she had access to information

from other prisons and if she could, please, see if she could find him somewhere else.

"I went through the entire state of Washington system," she said, in a tone that added, *of course*. "There is no Derrick Horn currently in the Washington State prison system."

I thanked her for her time and left, my mind a blank. Now you see him, now you don't.

I got back in my car and headed on down 101 toward Olympia, puzzling over the news I'd just been given. If the man had entered prison over fifteen years ago, Mikah must still have been in the womb. So had he been taken to visit his father when he was younger? Or did he know him only through his letters? But wouldn't the postmarks on those letters show Mikah that his father was no longer in Shelton?

And if Horn had been returned to court to face other charges, what were they? Had the man he assaulted died? Was he tried for murder? But wouldn't that be double jeopardy? And even if he'd been acquitted of murder, wouldn't the original charges still hold? Why wouldn't he show up in the system after those first five months?

And then there was Astrid. Why had she given her permission for what was essentially a wild-goose chase? A little passive–aggressive put-down for the nosy interloper? Did she know where Horn was now? If so, I thought, she was unlikely to tell the self-same snoop.

As though I didn't have trouble enough with my own case, I fretted. This mini-mystery was an aggravation I could do without. Maybe, I hoped, Simon would be able to set the Bercain case back on track and improve my tolerance for side issues. And the trip was, after all, getting me out of temptation's way with Jake.

CHAPTER
29

URSULA AND HARRY POUND are the unmatched pair of caretakers for Simon's house and grounds—a modest estate, but comfortable. Harry is a little on the dumpy and unlettered side for an English butler, but Simon enjoys the fiction. And Ursula has a voice that shivers timbers, but she cooks like a goddess, so Simon tolerates them both to run his household.

"Molly Piper!" Ursula bellowed from the open doorway, before Simon's portly frame appeared behind her and came around to wrap me in his usual bear hug. I sighed at the pleasure of being embraced without strings.

Later, in the living room, after I'd unloaded my anguish about Gray and my frustration with the case and my life in general (I didn't mention my night with Jake, only his presence in Free's house), he filled me in on his computer search on my behalf.

"Believe it or not," Simon said, "Flora Nightingale is the lady's real name. Daughter of Ballard and Evelyn Nightingale, born in St. Francisville, Louisiana, thirty-two years ago. Two years of junior college, then hostess at the Cajun Queen in Baton Rouge, promoted to assistant manager of the New Orleans franchise."

He set that paper of notes aside and picked up another. "No more on her until three years later she shows up as assistant manager of The Riverboat in Seattle, a restaurant owned by the Hors d'Oeuvres Corporation. Which just happens to also own—"

"The Queen's Rest," I said.

"Give the little lady a glass of champagne." Simon picked up the bottle of chardonnay we'd been drinking and refilled my glass.

"And these are all just restaurants?" I asked.

"The Cajun Queen, apparently yes. But The Riverboat was raided last year for gambling and suspicion of prostitution. They couldn't make it stick, but that's when Ms. Nightingale drops from the payroll and shows up at The Queen's Rest."

"Enterprising lady. But does any of it link her to Bercain?"

"I thought you'd never ask. I let my digits do the strolling through the corporate structure of Hors D'Oeuvres, Incorporated, and guess who turns out to have been vice president in charge of public relations in Seattle until three years ago?"

"Ah. The sauce thickens." I took another sip of wine. The lunch—of angel-hair pasta with shrimp and hot French bread—the mellow wine, and especially the company were bringing my anxiety level steadily down. "Any trace of Bercain in The Queen's Rest structure?"

"None I could find."

"So Kendall's spotting the two there could have been business or pleasure or both."

"So it would seem."

"When I get back I'm going to dig into everything I can find out about that damn white house. My gut tells me that Bercain was involved somehow in that whole operation. I saw both his campaign manager and his bank insider there, clinking glasses with Ms. Nightingale. Bercain's sticky fingers must have been in there somewhere. Anything bell-ringing about any of the others?"

"Not so far. But I have several other sources to check out."

"Thanks. What would I do without you, Simon?"

"Learn computers."

"Only the smallest part of your value to me, and you know it."

"Happy to be of service."

"Simon?"

"Ma'am?"

"You never speak of your private life, and I've never asked."

"For which I thank you."

"Oh. So don't ask?"

"What did you want to know?"

"Your past life, I guess. Did you ever marry, have children?"

"The marriage didn't last and did not encourage others."

I was silent, hoping he would continue but not wanting to pry.

Simon shifted his weight in his favorite brown leather chair. Each time I visited he seemed to have put on a few more pounds. Not obese by any means, just the logical result of a love for good food and drink, without seeing much reason to busy his body.

"A tawdry tale, not worth telling."

I kept waiting, hoping he'd go on. As often happened after one of Ursula's meals, I was lying on my back on the vicuña rug before the fire, near the footrest of Simon's chair. The fireplaces in the aged Tudor burned coal, not wood, but it was still too close for comfort to the night before.

"She came, she conquered, she left," Simon said. "A *short* tawdry tale."

"I'm sorry."

"It was a long time ago."

"And there weren't other women after?"

"Neither fore nor aft. I decided it was something I was not good at. I try to go with my strengths."

"I can't imagine anything you're not good at."

"The lady is gracious."

"Do you know that you're the only man alive I would let call me a *lady*?" I held up an imaginary cup with my pinky in the air.

"An honor, I'm sure."

I stared into the fire. Lady. Right. I'd have liked to talk to Simon about what happened with Jake, but he had just made it clear that it was not his area of expertise. Whose, I wondered, was it? Obviously not mine.

Instead, I said, "You know the guy I was supposed to visit this morning in prison?"

"The father of your young friend."

"Yes. He wasn't there. Hadn't been for fifteen years."

"What gave you reason to think he would be?"

"His son has been getting letters from him there. And when I asked the mother if I could visit, since she wouldn't let her son, she didn't say, 'No, the man's not there.' "

"Would she know? For certain?"

"You'd think so."

"Were they married?"

"She goes by his name."

"And the boy is his?"

"Yes. There's a sister who's not. Father unknown, Mikah says, according to the mother."

"Sibling rivalry?"

"No. The two are devoted to each other. Them against the world, I think. The mother's gone a lot of the time. Now I guess I know why."

"And the prison wouldn't say where he'd gone?"

"Back to Seattle to stand trial for some other crime was all they knew."

"Hmmm."

The next morning I was greeted with more than Ursula's luscious walnut waffles. Simon had, he said, located Derrick Horn. In the *federal* prison system. At Sheridan, in Oregon, to be exact.

His crime?

"Grand theft."

"That's a federal crime?"

"This one, apparently. Federal property, a payroll perhaps, something taken across state lines—there are a number of possibilities."

I chewed my bite of waffle, followed it with a handful of grapes. "How far south is Sheridan?"

"About two-thirds of the way to Salem, halfway west to the coast."

"Not a far drive, now that I've come this far." I munched some more. "But they probably wouldn't let me see him, any more than they would at Shelton."

"I may be able to help you there," Simon said, stirring cream into his coffee. "The warden there went through training with me at Quantico."

I stared at him. "You were once a fed?"

He smiled enigmatically. "The training only."

"What happened?"

"I decided not to join the club."

"I can't quite picture you as a fed."

"Ultimately, neither could I. We went our separate ways."

"And your friend?"

"He went into the agency, stayed awhile, then switched to the correctional system."

"And now he's the warden at Sheridan?"

"Last I heard. Shall I call and find out?"

"Yes, please. That'd be great!"

He called. His friend was still the warden. He agreed to let me visit his prisoner. Apparently, a warden can overrule an inmate with regard to visitors.

I arrived at 10:05 that morning, was told the visiting hours didn't begin until 4:45 that afternoon. My status as a private investigator seemed to carry no weight here either.

"My colleague spoke to the warden, though, just this morning. He said to come ahead."

The guard looked unmoved.

"Actually, it's my understanding that he preferred I come when other visitors wouldn't be there."

That at least got me in the door.

The male receptionist, whose only difference from the guards seemed to be his perfectly pressed charcoal suit and white dress shirt, gave me a skeptical look and connected himself to the warden's office.

Apparently my understanding was confirmed, because he called over the same guard, who'd been standing back near the front door, and told him to take me to the visitors' room. The receptionist buzzed us through the locked inner double doors.

The young guard walked ramrod-straight, wearing a huge ring of keys on one hip and a walkie-talkie on the other. The guards didn't carry guns, he answered to my question. Too tempting to be seized and used against them. I told him I seldom did either, for the same reason.

He stared at me, the look I was used to. "You *are* a private investigator? Really?"

I crossed my heart and held up three fingers in the Girl Scout promise. He didn't crack a smile.

The room he ushered me into was huge, full of gray metal tables and gray metal chairs. The institutional-green walls could have enclosed any school cafeteria.

The guard gestured toward one of the chairs and I sat, staring at the empty one across a small table from me. Suddenly I felt shy, like a kid on his first day at school. I wished there were other visitors in the room.

I ran a hand through my bushy hair, thinking how

unlikely a reputable adult I would appear to Mikah's father. I should have worn a skirt. Maybe, I thought, I should identify myself professionally, present my license or something. But then he'd see me as part of the law-enforcement troops that had him surrounded.

My decision-making ended as the guard returned, prodding ahead of him a short, stocky man with black hair and a thick mustache, his wrists cuffed in front of him. He looked nothing like the man whose photograph Mikah had shown me.

The guard thrust him down onto the chair that faced mine and backed off, but not more than ten feet away.

"Mr. Horn," I said, fighting the impulse to stick out my hand to shake his. "I'm Molly Piper. I'm a friend of your son, Mikah. He's been wanting to visit you, but his mother hasn't wanted him to . . . go so far from home, so I've come instead."

The man's flat brown eyes showed no reaction.

"Actually," I said, "I thought you were at Shelton. Mikah, that is, thought that's where you were."

He said nothing.

"From your letters, I guess."

Nothing.

I backtracked. "I met Mikah only recently, but I've been very impressed by him. He's a sweet boy, and so talented. I first met him when we were making luminarias for the New Year's parade. Those are Spanish candles, sort of," I added, in case he didn't recognize the term.

Horn's frown became a scowl. "Makah is Indian, not Spanish."

"I know he's Makah," I said quickly. "As you are."

"His name," Horn growled. "*Mah*-kah, not *My*-kah. Is that what he calls himself? He should be proud he's Makah, not try to be some white boy."

The man's speech had been impassioned, lifting the cloud from his eyes for a moment. He glared at me, then dropped his gaze.

"He *is* proud," I retorted, the volume of my voice rising in frustration. I hadn't expected to have to defend Mikah to his father. "He's *very* proud of his Indian heritage. And of you. He's done such a remarkable job of reproducing those artifacts you found."

Horn's gaze snapped up. "He showed you those?"

Just what his wife had said, I remembered. "Yes, in his room. With all the pictures of his Makah relatives."

My mind was beginning to pull me in a direction I really didn't want to go. "Your letters too," I said, with failing conviction.

Horn's stare was blank.

"You haven't been writing him." My voice sounded just as dull.

He turned belligerent, gesturing with his chin at the surroundings. "What would I do that for? You see anything around here he needs to know? Better he forget his loser father. Like his mother says."

"Am I understanding correctly?" I said slowly. "You were sent to Shelton for assault and battery?"

"The asshole deserved it."

"That was on your dig?"

Horn shifted his weight in the flimsy chair. "Us native kids did all the heavy work. Every summer. For nothing. They got all the glory, all the money. Then they'd have taken our treasures too."

"So you've been here how long?"

He scowled. "*Fifteen years.*"

"Fifteen years for a single assault?"

He glared at the floor. "Some guards too; they had it coming. And there are some on that parole board I'd like to . . ."

"Mr. Horn, how long has it been since you saw your son?"

He glared at me, raised his manacled hands. "I told you, I don't want no son of mine to see me like this."

"Have you *ever* seen him, written to him?"

Horn averted his gaze for some time before he said, "When his mother found out she was carrying him, she wanted us to get married, there in the jail, so he wouldn't be a bastard. I wrote him a letter then, told him to be proud of his heritage, of being a Makah." His black eyes returned to mine, burning with belligerence. "He comes from a proud people."

I put my hand to the ache in my throat. "Yes," I said. "And he needs that pride so much, he's been making it up. Your letters, your role in the discovery of the artifacts. He told me you were an archaeologist, that they were your finds."

That brought a near-grin to the heavy face. "He's learning to lie, that's good. It will help him survive."

I leaned forward over the table, saw the guard's stance become more alert. "Mr. Horn, your son is fifteen years old now. Every boy needs his father at this time in his life. Even if you're still in here. If you want me to and can persuade your wife, I'll bring him to see you myself. But at least he needs you to write to him. Tell him what it is to be a proud young Native American. I don't know exactly what's going on at his school, but I know he's considered at-risk. Tell him how important it is that he get an education, so he doesn't—"

Horn's gaze sharpened. "—end up like me," he finished the sentence.

I lowered my voice. "The artifacts are real, aren't they? You took them. That's why you're in a federal prison, for stealing from a national site."

Horn leaped to his feet. "I didn't steal nothing! They belong to my people! I am keeping them for my people! It is my son's duty to guard them, keep them safe from the white man! *That's* what I have told him."

The guard had shot to him when he first stood, gripped him from behind with an arm around his neck. Now he began dragging him back toward the door.

"My son is Makah!" Horn shouted.

"So tell him!" I shouted back. "Write to him!"

Then the door clanged behind them and the room was silent, holding only the echoes of our voices. I put my fingertips to my perspiring temples, felt my pulse beat there. Why hadn't I suspected that the artifacts were real? Because I'd automatically believed Mikah? A pro investigator never automatically believes anyone. I'd let my affection for the boy blind me to what was right before my eyes. So what else had I been blind to? Who else's story had I swallowed whole? Kendall's? Denny's? Dorothy's? Amber's? Maia's? And worst of all: Jake's?

CHAPTER
30

I DIDN'T GO BACK along the Hood River; I went straight up I-5 to Emerald, to the home of Timothy Gray.

I thought I might have to use my key and wait for him; it was only four-thirty. But he opened the door.

We stood staring at each other, like high-noon gunmen waiting for the other to draw.

"Can I come in?" I said finally, and he broke his stance, stepped back to let me enter.

"It's good to see you," he said, closing the door.

I thought I detected a limp. He looked pale and even thinner than usual.

"You're sick," I said.

He gave the barest nod and extended his arm toward the living room.

I sat on the couch; he sat in his usual leather recliner. On a tray table beside it were pill bottles. Lots of them. And one of those oversize pink-tinted plastic holders with the letters of the week stamped on top.

Chemotherapy.

"Where is it?" I said, my voice coming out a toneless croak.

"The groin."

I closed my eyes. No wonder he'd been avoiding sex; I'd have been able to detect it.

Detect. How lousy a detective did that make me? There'd probably been signs. If I'd wanted to see them.

Denial.

I felt a rivulet of water run down my jaw to my chin. I hadn't even known I was crying.

I swiped it off roughly as grief turned to anger. "So why the hell didn't you *tell* me?"

He shrugged. "What could you have done?"

"How long have you been on chemotherapy?"

"The Monday after I last saw you."

"So you thought I should run off and play while you put yourself through this hell?" My gesture encompassed the pills and his body.

"Basically, yes. There was no need for you to go through this too."

"Whose 'no need'? Didn't you ever think I might *want* to? Because I *love* you? Because I'd want to do everything I possibly could to help you through this?"

My anger was gaining momentum. It felt better than the deep ache filling my chest. "Dammit, Gray, I knew you were treating me like a child; I just didn't know why!"

He said simply, "I wanted to spare you this. It isn't fun."

What he should be saying, I thought, was that if I were the mature adult I wanted to be taken for, I'd have *seen* it.

I coughed to try to dislodge the constriction in my throat. "What's the prognosis?"

He shrugged. "Who's to say? Apparently it was busy spreading while I was busy policing."

At least we shared the guilt of denial. But I stayed on the offensive. "What's the damn *prognosis*?"

He smiled at me with some of the old indulgence. "It's good to have your spirit back in my life."

That did it. That broke the dam. He moved to the couch and held me while I convulsed with sobs.

"I'm moving in," I said finally.

"There's no need—" he began, but my look stopped him.

"My current case is winding up," I said, trying not to think *how* it was winding up. "Then I'll move in, give you some proper care until you're well again." I avoided eye contact while I said this. We would pretend that could be the prognosis.

He didn't object.

"And please tell me you're *not* still playing Big Chief on the side," I said, rising. It's hard to be assertive from down there.

"I'm on a leave of absence," Gray said.

"Good. Then I'll have you all to myself."

He smiled wryly. "What's left of me," he said, a weariness in his voice I'd never heard before.

"There's plenty left," I told him hotly. "You could lose half yourself and still be more than the top ten people in the universe." It was the truth.

He smiled. "I do love you," he said.

"No more than I love you."

That, too, was the truth.

CHAPTER
31

BACK IN GRACE I went straight to the library, clicked on the Sno-Isle system, and entered *Makah Indians* as subject.

Eight titles came up, with 970 or 979 codings.

Only two were shown to be currently in the Grace branch, but it didn't take much thumbing through them to find many of the "photographs" on Mikah's walls. The "uncle" making the mask, wearing the medal; the "father," who turned out to be the head of the tribal council at the time of the dig and looked nothing at all like the man I'd just seen in Sheridan prison.

My heart ached as I turned the pages of Mikah's fantasy. A family found in a book.

Pictures of the artifacts in Mikah's room were also there: the harpoon; the seal club, with its rough profile of a seal, which became a mournful human face when seen from above. At least, I thought grimly, Mikah has had the originals of those all his life.

I set off for Chief Belgium's office, hoping I could still catch him in.

As I pushed on the glass door going in, Bernie Wu appeared, pushing out. We did the after-you bowing thing, then I went on through. The chief's office was empty; apparently he'd left at his usual five o'clock sharp.

Bernie finished shoving a wad of prints into a manila envelope.

"Are those the New Year's Eve photos, by chance?" I asked sweetly.

"In fact, yes," he said, holding the envelope closer to his chest. "The chief left them for me with Suki."

Suki Klein was the night operator of the East Island Emergency System; the shift changed at five.

"Can I see?" I said, as Bernie lifted them higher. He's not that much taller than I am, and I began gauging whether I could jump high enough to grab them. "Come on," I said, "it's not as though I'm out to publish them before you do. Bercain was my client."

Reluctantly, Bernie handed them to me. I shuffled through, looking for any in the neighborhood of Bercain's attack. But there were none.

Bernie saw my disappointment and, with a sigh, drew one out of the breast pocket of his soccer shirt. "This what you're looking for?" he said. "This is the only one close to Daisy, and I guess we'll print it; but if it means something to you, you'll have it all over the rest of us."

The Last Diner was in the background of the shot, but the only person in evidence was nearly off the right edge of the print—a figure in a black cape with a lump on its back, passing close to the camera. Only a sliver of its mask could be seen, but I remembered seeing it that night: a long white, twisted face, its mouth open in anguish.

" 'The Scream,' " I said. "Munch's painting 'The Scream.' "

"Give the girl an M.F.A.," Bernie said. "Belgium's been questioning every artist in town—which is going some. See if anybody had a grudge against Bercain. Or if they saw anything. Only in Grace, right? Dress up as some esoteric painting."

Suki was passing on her way to the bathroom and looked over Bernie's shoulder. "That's *Scream*," she said.

"What is?"

"The mask. From that teen slasher movie *Scream*. Very big the last few Halloweens."

But I had begun to see something else, a similarity to another face. And there was something sticking out of the hump. I peered closer.

"What?" Bernie said.

"Katum," I whispered to myself. "Costume."

"What?"

I handed the photo back to him. "I've gotta go," I said, already moving toward the door.

He was sitting on his rock, staring at The Faces. He looked up as I dropped to the sand and watched intently as I approached.

I waited until I was seated on what had become my rock, next to his. "I found your father," I said.

"I knew you would."

"He's not at Shelton."

"All my letters came back."

I told him where his father was and why. "I hope he'll write to you," I said, though I found very little hope in my heart.

A long silence stretched between us before I said, "I know they're real."

"I knew you would," he repeated. His face was closed again, like a mask.

"He left them with you, with your mother for you to keep."

"For the tribe. For our people. He said they were all he had to give me."

"I have to see them again."

He nodded, his face impassive. Then he got up and

followed him across the beach to the steps and we started the climb.

As we approached the apartment, Astrid Horn burst from the back door, attractively dressed in a long ruby velvet dress and heels, her hair upswept above a black taffeta cape. "Where have you *been*?" she snapped at Mikah, without breaking stride. "I'm late for my date and Emily is on a tear."

She frowned a little when she noticed me but kept going toward her car. I noticed that it had a new passenger door, which almost matched the rest of its body.

We heard Emily's screech before we even opened the door. She was sitting in the middle of the kitchen table, food and broken dishes scattered around her. She held half a banana in her right hand, a strip of peeling in her left, which she had raised as though about to throw it. At the sight of Mikah, her screech wound down like an ambulance siren reaching its destination, and she dropped the peel.

"Emily," Mikah said, his voice sounding as weary as an old man's. "Give it a rest."

The child gave me a hard look. "Danger," she said.

"It's all right, Emily," Mikah mumbled, passing the table.

The child slid off with a thud and followed her brother. I brought up the rear.

There was a padlock affixed to the knob on Mikah's bedroom door. I'd noticed it before, inside on his desk. Had he removed it while I was downstairs looking at the mail the last time?

He turned the key, pulled the padlock off the hasp, and opened the door. The room looked a bit more tidy than it had before but otherwise the same. I went straight to the foot of the bed, where the club still lay on a pair of nails against the wall. I leaned toward its bulbous tip, the snub nose and slanted eye Mikah had identified as the head of a seal. And the mournful face they made on top.

"Ka-tum," Emily said again.

I didn't have to look too hard. There was evidence of a piece splintered off one side. I suspected I would find it in the pocket of my slicker. And there were bits of hair stuck to the raw open grain of the head. Stuck with a dark rusty substance that had to be blood.

"It's okay," Mikah said behind me. "I knew you'd find out."

I turned to face him. "Why?"

Mikah's gaze lowered from mine. "You think I don't know about my mother? He did that, got her into that."

"How do you know?"

"It was his place. First that one on the hill, above Port Angel, then the new one on Sunflower. He kept saying there'd be a market for that in Grace."

Head down, Mikah kicked one boot against the metal frame of his bed. I wondered if that was the one that had left the print at the playground. Had he deposited Emily there while he did the deed?

"The creep used to be her boyfriend, sort of," he mumbled, "when he first got here. He wasn't such a big shot then. He came sniffing around. We started eating better. But he wouldn't take her out in public, he had his eyes on bigger game. When his engagement to that other woman got announced, she went ballistic. He didn't come around anymore, but that's when she started going out at night, all dressed up like that."

He made a snorting noise. "I followed her one night, to that Queen's place. I thought, maybe she's just going there hoping he might be there and see her and fall in love with her again." He gave the bed another kick. "Loser!"

I didn't know whether he meant his mother, Bercain, or himself. Maybe all three.

"He never came around here anymore. When she

started showing, she said she didn't know whose it was. By that time I believed her. She always came back smelling like—you know."

I didn't say anything. Mikah seemed to need to unload. I found myself wondering when and why he'd picked me to uncover his truth. Miss Marple/Mother Confessor.

"Then right before last Christmas, I saw them. Well, heard them. At that restaurant, The Galleon. I was out back, where the Dumpster is. And the vents."

He looked at me a bit defensively. "Sometimes you can find good stuff there. Better'n the stuff she feeds us.

"She was telling him she needed money for presents. For Emily. She says, 'Your own child.' He says, 'How do I know that, all the men you been with?' She says, 'You know, all right. I wasn't with nobody else till you left me. I was already pregnant.' "

Mikah looked at me again. "I believed her."

I touched his hand. "Don't tell me any more. You need a lawyer. Don't talk to anybody, the police, anybody, without a lawyer present. You don't want to give the impression of too much . . . premeditation."

"I don't care," he said sullenly, turning around to look at Emily, who was sitting quite still now on the bed, watching him. "Maybe she'll have to be a real mother now. I'll tell them about that place she goes, they'll shut it down."

I walked Mikah down to City Hall. I'd phoned, and Chief Belgium said he'd meet us there. Mikah carried Emily piggyback, while I carried the club, protected from my fingerprints with toilet paper. I said I'd take Emily with me afterward, until their mother got home. I'd left a note on the kitchen table, with Free's phone number. I knew that meant I'd have to stay there, but I had to talk to Jake anyway. If only I knew what to say.

I'd called Eugene, my downstairs neighbor. He said he had no experience in criminal law but recommended someone, said he'd call her, have her meet us there or come himself.

Mikah told essentially the same story he'd told me regarding motive, but he skirted the long-term premeditation issue under the direction of Yulanda Paris. Yes, he said, Emily had been there, on his back, carrying the club. I saw Belgium's eyes narrow at that: He'd brought the weapon. Mikah said he'd set Emily down at the vacant People's Park at Dandelion and Daisy, told her to wait there for him.

Initially, he said, he'd only meant to talk to Bercain. He'd seen him through the window in The Last Diner and waited for him to come out. Bercain suggested they move away from the crowd.

All he wanted, Mikah said, was some regular support for Emily, so his mother wouldn't have to do what she was doing. But Bercain brushed him off, told him to "get lost. Your mother was a whore long before I met her."

That's when Mikah lost it, he said. He didn't know how many times he'd hit Bercain. "A lot."

Then Belgium's second round of questioning was interrupted by an incoming call on the emergency line.

"Third block of Sunflower," I heard Suki say, speaking to Herb Longstreth, head of Grace's volunteer fire squad. "That big white house down the cliff."

The picture that popped into my mind was of Kendall Bercain's long fingers tearing a match from a glossy white matchbook embossed with a golden nightingale.

Or maybe someone's mother decided to eliminate it as a temptation.

Or maybe it was just an accident.

But I didn't think so. I wondered whether Denny would go down with them.

It was nearly eleven when I got home, but the lights were still on at Free's. I took a deep breath and carried

Emily inside. She'd finally fallen asleep in Belgium's office and didn't wake when I'd transferred her to my car. But she began screaming when I lifted her out.

Jake was in the kitchen in his wheelchair, held out his arms when he saw her, and she settled back to sleep in his lap.

I filled Jake in on what had happened. "Sonofabitch," he growled a couple of times, about Bercain's activities, then, "Good for him" at the story of Mikah's actions.

I sat at the table, drained of energy and suffused with sadness. "Not good for him," I said. "He'll go to prison. What kind of shape is he going to be in when he gets out of there? It can't be good."

And what about Emily, I thought. She was now left without the person closest to her. What would she be told about where her brother was? Or the identity of her father? And would her mother really be there for her now any more than she'd been before? There was only despair in the thought of Emily following in any of their footsteps.

Jake, too, had fallen silent. We sat for quite a while in our separate thoughts, before I raised my head and looked at him. He was beautiful, really, I thought, holding the sleeping child, his dark hair and beard highlighted with gold by the stained-glass lamp hanging above him.

Then he felt my look and raised his head. His dark eyes glowed, but from what combination of emotions I would probably never know.

"You're very beautiful," I said.

That brought a look of amazement, then amusement. Then his face turned grave again. "You too," he said, studying me carefully. "You're going back to him, aren't you?" His voice was low and resigned.

"Yes," I said, thinking there was little point in detailing the separation or the reunion. "It has nothing—" I started, but he cut me off.

"No need to explain," he said. "I'm a big boy."

"Big enough to love again?" I'd said it before I could edit the presumptuous question.

But he seemed to take no offense. "I could have loved you," he said.

"Me too," I said and meant it.

We looked at each other. Then he said, "Fate stinks."

Thinking of Gray, of Jake, of Emily and Mikah, even his father and mother, I could not disagree.

EPILOGUE

I STOOD BESIDE CHIEF BELGIUM, watching a pair of gray-clad guards lead Mikah in handcuffs toward a van marked MEACHUM CORRECTION CENTER. "I'll come see you soon," I called. Again.

"It's a pretty good place," Belgium said. "He was lucky not to get tried as an adult."

We watched as the guards boosted the boy into the back of the van.

"He can get help there," Belgium said. "Hopefully."

"Yeah," I said past the rock in my throat. "Hopefully."

About the Author

PATRICIA BROOKS was fiction editor of the *Northwest Review* literary magazine while in the three-year MFA program at the University of Oregon. Adventures before and since have included seven years in New York City as a film and drama critic, a decade as a political journalist/activist, and three years as head gardener on a commune in Virginia. She is now permanently settled on the island that is the model for Prince Island, and intends to follow Molly through many more mysteries.